Alpha Claimed

Sometimes Choosing the right Mate can change the Fate of an entire Kingdom

USA TODAY BESTSELLING AUTHOR

REBEKAH R. GANIERE

Alpha Claimed

Rebekah R. Ganiere

ISBN: 978-1-63300-089-6

ISBN: 978-1-63300-090-2

All ARTWORK by VWZDesigns.com

DEDICATION

To those who Read, and to those who Love, and those who love to do both.

CHAPTER ONE

RIVER

River sat at a large, highly polished wooden table. At one head seat sat Ares, and on the opposite side, Apollo sat in the head seat. River sat between them, with over five seats on either side of her. Across from her sat three older Lycans, all members of the Elder Council. The men stared at her, making her wolf pace uncomfortably.

"May I call you River, Highness?" asked one Elder.

"No," Ares and Apollo said together.

The tension in the air grew so thick that River didn't think she could have bitten through it with her fangs.

Her wolf whined, looking from Ares to Apollo and back again.

"Highness," repeated the Elder. "I am Osmodius, High Elder and uncle to Ares and Apollo. I welcome you to our lands and your new home."

River nodded and fiddled with the seam on her jeans.

"Highness, can you please try to explain what you are feeling?"

"Confused."

He nodded. "I'm sure you are. We all are."

"Is it even possible?" she asked. "That I could be both of their mates?"

Osmodius looked between the brothers and sighed. "It's... not unheard of, but it's exceedingly rare. But then, so are identical twins."

Ares slammed his fist into the table. "This is bullshit. She's mine. She said she's mine. I know she's mine."

Osmodius held up his hand. "I understand. But it is possible that you are not the only one she is right for."

"Tell them," Ares said. "Tell them you are mine, Beloved."

River looked at her hands. "It's true I did accept Ares."

"But he hasn't marked her," Apollo said. "That means the bond hasn't been completed."

River didn't like the pit that grew in her stomach as each moment passed.

"It's only because, due to my status, we knew that it was important to do things in the traditional manner," said Ares.

"But it hasn't been completed," Apollo said again.

Ares growled, and she glanced up at him. More than anything, she wished she could feel the comfort of his touch. As if sensing her distress, he stood and stepped toward her.

Apollo stood as well and growled. "Don't."

"Let's not get blood on your mother's favorite table, please," said Osmodius.

The brothers looked at each other, and then they both sat at the same time.

Identical faces. Identical mannerisms. Identical personalities.

Great. Just great. River didn't have just one overbearing Alpha to deal with; she had two. She wanted to run away. To get on her motorcycle and ride back to New York.

Oh, wait. She didn't have her motorcycle. *Dammit.*

Man… when her mom found out…

She sighed.

"I think there is only one good way to settle this," said Osmodius. "We must let Her Highness decide which mate to take."

She looked to Ares. He smiled at her in triumph.

Ares. She chose Ares.

"Wait!" Apollo yelled. "It's not fair. He's had an entire week with her. She doesn't know me at all. If you make her choose now, I don't stand a chance."

"Then I challenge you for her," said Ares.

"Wow!" said Apollo. "You are willing to give her up so easily, brother?"

Ares' fangs descended. "No. I'm ready to kill you to have her."

"Enough," said Osmodius. "The choice must be Her Highness's. But Apollo is right. To make her choose now would be unfair. Therefore, we will give her one month to make a decision. One month to spend with both of you and decide between you."

"That still gives him the advantage," said Apollo. "He's already had a week with her. Her bond with him is stronger. How can I compete with that?"

"If you don't think you can win her over, you can always relinquish your claim now."

"Not on your life," Apollo growled.

Osmodius looked at the other two elders, and they nodded.

"Very well. We will give Apollo one additional week to spend with her."

"Alone," said Apollo.

Ares jumped to his feet. "Absolutely not."

"What? Are you afraid that, away from your Alpha-hole ways, she might pick me?"

Ares grabbed the table's edge, and River could feel him hanging on by a thread.

"All right," she said.

All eyes turned to her.

"I'll do it. I'll spend time with Prince Apollo for four days."

"A week," Apollo corrected.

"Ares and I didn't spend a full week together in New York. He had meetings most days and was gone quite a bit." She wasn't about to tell Apollo or the elders that he'd moved into a different hotel room for four of the days and that she'd hidden from him for a day and a half.

"And she had a guard with her at all times. I want Zeke to go with them."

"No," said Apollo. "We'll take Silas and Bennett."

"No," Ares bellowed.

"Five days," said Osmodius. "You may pick which days-"

"Now," said Apollo. "Right now."

"She's just arrived and needs time to adjust," said Ares.

"Which is why it should be right now. Before she gets too cozy with you here at the estate." Apollo looked to Osmodius.

"I'd like Lachlan to come," River said. "Zeke and Bianca are trying to settle things back in the States so she can move here. I wouldn't want to take him away from her. But Lachlan… I would feel comfortable if he came." She hoped that her inference about how Apollo was taking her away so soon wouldn't go unnoticed.

"I would be honored," Lachlan stepped forward.

"Agreed," the other two said in unison.

"Where are you taking her?" Ares asked.

"Why? You gonna show up?"

"No. Because someone should know where she is in case you don't bring her back."

"We will make sure he leaves the address with us," said Osmodius.

"Fine. But at least let her eat before leaving," said Ares. "She hasn't eaten in hours."

"We can get something on the way." Apollo stood. "And no need to pack; we can get whatever we need when we get there."

River's heart hammered, and her hands shook. They talked about her like she wasn't even in the room, and that she wouldn't have. Yes, they may have just decided that she had to spend time with Apollo, but her life was still her own, and if she wanted to, she could just walk out the door and tell them all to screw themselves, and there was nothing they could do about it.

"I want to eat now," she blurted. "And change my clothes. And pee."

The men looked at her, and Osmodius nodded. "Of course, Highness. Take as long as you need."

"One hour," said Apollo.

"Two," she countered. "If I am about to go to an undisclosed location in a foreign country with a man I don't even know, the least you can do is give me two hours to prepare."

"Agreed," said one of the elders.

Her shoulders relaxed a fraction.

Osmodius looked at his watch. "Very well. Please be ready by five p.m., Highness."

Apollo burst from the room and disappeared. River waited until the three elders left before running to Ares and being swept into his arms. He kissed her head, and she held back a sob. Just when she'd gotten used to the idea of being his mate, she had to start all over again with someone else. It felt worse than cheating. Despite Apollo's pull on her wolf, she'd already made her choice.

"I don't want to go."

Ares kissed her hair again and pulled her even closer. "I don't want you to."

"Why do I have to go with him? Why can't they just let us be?"

Ares stiffened. "Because... He is the Alpha of Alphas."

She stepped back and looked up at him. "The what?"

Ares blew out a breath. "The Alpha of Alphas. When more than one Alpha is born into the family, it falls on the oldest to take charge. He was given the title of Alpha of Alphas."

"But... you're twins."

"And he's five minutes older."

"Five minutes? Are you joking? They are basing all of this on five minutes?" The fate of her future came down to Apollo evacuating his mother's womb first.

"I am not the Alpha of Alphas. I am only second in line. Therefore, they have to give him a chance. They have no choice. Alphas need mates, and their mates need to bear pups. Apollo and I are way past the age where we should have found you. As much as I hate it with every hair on my body, they must give him a chance. If you are indeed his fated mate as you are mine, then not giving him a chance would go against everything we believe in."

"But... I don't want him," she whispered.

Ares cupped her face and kissed her. "Believe me, I don't want you to want him, Beloved."

ARES

Ares tried to keep from losing it in front of River. Just the thought of her alone in the company of another male, especially his brother, scared him more than words could describe.

His whole life, Apollo had tried to take everything Ares cared about. Their father's affection. Then their mother's. And now his fated mate's.

They lay on his bed, wrapped in each other's arms, listening to the clock ticking on the wall. She'd not spoken in almost thirty minutes, and the tension in her posture told him everything he needed to know.

"Tell me something about yourself," she said into his chest. "Something... special."

Special? What was special about him?

He thought for a moment. "When I was young, I used to have a favorite blanket. I took it everywhere with me. One day, it disappeared. I was devastated. My mother had made me the blanket out of her nightgowns."

River squeezed him. "Do you know what happened to it?"

"I have a pretty good idea." *Apollo.*

A knock on the door pulled their attention, and Ares looked at the clock. Four fifty-five.

"Come," he called.

Lachlan opened the door and peeked inside. "It's time, Highnesses."

"We're coming."

His wolf snarled and paced so hard that every ounce of his body focused on not shifting.

"I should go," she said. "I don't want to make him mad."

Ares tipped her chin, so she looked at him. "Who cares if it does?"

"I don't want him to hurt you again."

"If he hurts *you* in any way, I will kill him. Elders or no elders."

She gave him a sad smile and then slid off the bed. Ares rose as well, but she stopped him.

"No. I don't want you to see this."

"River-"

She ran to him, slammed her lips into his, and quickly broke away.

"I should have let you mark me. I should have asked you last night."

His heart shattered at her confession, and he pulled her close. "No, Beloved. We both know that you would have regretted it later if you had. This is better."

Her eyes narrowed. "You don't mean that."

Did he? "I do," he finally said. "This way, when you choose me, there will be no doubt in your mind."

CHAPTER TWO

APOLLO

Apollo leaned against the back of his bike, his eyes trained on the front door. He sniffed the air and caught her scent growing closer.

Good.

His wolf paced and growled at the thoughts of what she and Ares might have been doing upstairs.

"Don't worry, boy, she'll be ours."

His wolf wasn't so sure. Ever since they'd been young, Ares had gotten everything Apollo had been rightly due. But not this time. A werewolf only got the chance for one fated mate, and he'd be damned if he'd let his brother take her from him as well.

River exited the front door and shielded her eyes from the bright sun. Lachlan showed her down the steps and met up with Silas and Bennett. The group walked toward him, and Apollo crossed his arms over his chest tighter to keep from reaching for her.

She wore jeans and boots with a loose T-shirt and hoodie. Even so, he couldn't take his eyes off her.

She stopped in front of him and looked over his bike.

"Have you ever been on a motorcycle before?"

She shrugged. "I've ridden a bit. Though I prefer my 1956 Uncle Pan to these new custom choppers."

His wolf howled, and Apollo couldn't help the smile that spread across his face.

Easy, boy.

"Good." He handed her a helmet, and she put it on without a word.

"Bennett, Silas, out front. Lachlan, pick up the rear in the car with the others."

The men nodded and headed to their vehicles.

Apollo straddled his bike and turned it on. River didn't move for a moment, and then her small form slid behind him. He gripped the handlebars tight at the feel of her so close. He waited for her arms to slide around his waist, but they didn't.

He chuckled. The woman was stubborn. No worries, though; she'd be clinging to him soon enough.

THEY'D BEEN RIDING FOR CLOSE TO FIFTEEN MINUTES WHEN RIVER grabbed onto his waist. The sensation sent a jolt of desire ripping through him. Apollo smiled as she squeezed her thighs around his and hooked her thumbs into his belt loops. Contact was good. Contact would help ease her reservations.

Unconsciously, he rubbed her hand until she removed it.

He tried to keep calm at the slight. Time. She just needed time. And that's what they'd get.

He pulled off the highway forty-five minutes later and slowed as he rode down Main Street. They passed several shops, and he pulled his bike to a stop.

"What do you wish to have for dinner?"

She stared at him through the helmet's visor. “I’ve already eaten. With Ares."

"Of course, but you'll be hungry again. So what do you prefer?"

She looked around at the shops. "Burger, fries, the largest cola they have."

A girl who really ate, there was nothing sexier.

He relayed the message to Bennett and then told him to get some staples before they took off again at a slower pace. Apollo let her look around as they rode through the rustic old town. More than once, he caught her checking out different sculptures they passed in the parks and town hall grounds.

So she likes art. He made a mental note to look into that.

They turned down a dirt road, and she grabbed him again as the ruts made their ride bumpier.

Finally, they came to a set of log cabins, and he pulled in front of the first one and stopped the bike. They were old, but he'd paid to keep them up, so the cabins weren't in bad shape. He had a specific reason for wanting to bring her there, and it was a bonus that there happened to be no cell or internet reception in the area.

She slid from the back of the bike and handed him her helmet before fluffing her long, silvery hair and stretching, revealing a good three inches of skin above her navel. Apollo's body hardened, and he coughed, looking away.

Don't be a dick, dick. If you can't even control yourself with a peek at just a few inches of skin, what will you do when you see more?

Lachlan approached them and addressed River, making Apollo want to rip his arms off.

"You all right, Highness?"

River rolled her eyes. "Lachlan-"

"I've tried. I swear I have, but I just can't."

"Okay, well then, Bodyguard, until you can call me by my first name, you shall henceforth and forward be known to me as Bodyguard."

Lachlan groaned. "Fine. R-"

"If you say her name, I'll rip your tongue out and eat it," said Apollo.

Lachlan blanched.

"Ares lets him call me River," she lied.

"Well, I am not my little brother. And my mate's name is reserved for my lips only. He may call you Highness, Princess, Omega, Luna, or Prince Apollo's intended, but neither he nor my men will call you by your birth name."

She held his gaze steadily for a moment, and her hands balled into fists. For a second, he imagined her trying to pummel him with those tiny little things. Instead, she turned and stomped toward the cabin, making his wolf chuff with each slight sway of her hips. As she went, Apollo swallowed hard and could practically see her tail swishing with anger. Man, he couldn't wait to meet her wolf.

APOLLO OPENED THE FRONT DOOR AS BENNETT AND SILAS ROLLED the bikes into the barn. He stepped aside while she entered and allowed her to take in the ample open space, while he took her in. He'd been unable to get a good look at her up to that point, so he took the opportunity while it lasted. She was petite and thin, but her walk told him she possessed a confidence that a shifter of her size rarely exuded. Instead, the small female shifters he'd known were more than content pretending to be weak to appeal to a male's protective mating instincts. But not River. No. If anything, she pretended to be stronger. He wondered what in her past made her that way.

She walked to the oversized fireplace and plucked a photograph from the mantel. She studied it for a moment and then put it back.

"So this is where you and Ares were born."

He wondered how she knew that from just looking at an old photo.

"It's where our ancestors first settled when they arrived in Montreal. Most young couples in our family spend time here in the beginning to connect with their roots."

She looked at him. "So now what? It's not like I have bags to unpack or anything."

"I hadn't thought that far ahead."

Her eyebrows scrunched together. "You don't know what we are doing?"

He shrugged. "What did you and Ares do?"

She swallowed hard and averted her eyes.

Interesting.

"We uh… went dancing. And to a museum and the theater. And I packed up my stuff. And he came to my show-"

"Your show?"

"I'm a sculptor."

"Clay?"

"Metal."

"That's hot."

She cocked an eyebrow at him.

"Get it. Because you have to melt the metal to bend it, and it gets hot?"

She shook her head, but he caught the hint of a smile on her lips, which made his wolf beg for more.

"How about we go for a run?"

She looked out the window. "It's not night yet."

He shrugged. "No one comes out here but family, which currently consists of me, my brother, my uncle Osmodius, his only living child, his daughter Amelia, and now you. So, I think we're good."

She looked out the window again, and he could practically hear her wolf begging to go.

Apollo stripped off his shirt and dropped it to the floor. "Tell ya what. I'm going for a run. If you care to join me, please do."

Her eyes glowed brighter as he kicked off his boots and undid his belt buckle. She blushed as he dropped his jeans to the floor and stood before her naked. He watched her expression change from curiosity to desire as the room grew heady with her scent.

"Uh, Highness?"

Apollo turned to find Lachlan standing, eyes wide at the door. Without explanation, he shifted midair, knocking Lachlan out of the way before he bounded down the steps and out into the trees.

CHAPTER THREE

RIVER

No. No. No. No. She had not just seen Apollo naked, and Lachlan had not walked in on it.

She covered her face as heat rose through her body, and her wolf yowled.

Stop! She told her wolf. *Don't think of him. Don't want him.*

Too late. Apollo had decided not to play fair, or maybe he'd just decided there was no use wasting time; either way, he'd just shown her the entire package. The entire beautifully tanned, ripped, muscular, and slightly larger package than Ares'.

"Highness?" Lachlan questioned. "Are you okay? I can get the car and have you out of here before he realizes we are gone."

She uncovered her heated face and looked at him. "Thank you, but I don't want you to be in the middle of… whatever this is."

He looked like he wanted to say something, but turned away instead.

"Lachlan?"

"Yes, Highness?"

"I... Uhm... I think I want to go for a run."

"Of course."

"Could you wait outside the door to open it for me after I've shifted?"

Lachlan bowed. “Certainly.”

"And Lachlan?"

He looked at her. "I appreciate you agreeing to come. I hate to put you in this position. I'm sure this is quite awkward for you."

He looked at her for a moment. "Significantly less than for you, I'm sure." He bowed. "I'll wait outside, Highness." He closed the door, and River swallowed hard before sinking into a well-loved denim couch.

She hung her head in her hands and then grabbed her phone from her hoodie pocket. She swiped the screen. She needed to hear Ares’ voice. She'd promised Apollo she'd spend time with him, but she'd never promised not to check in. Besides, Ares was probably already worried out of his mind.

She dialed the number he'd programmed into the phone and waited.

Nothing happened.

She tried again and again, but nothing happened. She looked at the screen. No signal. None at all. Not even one bar. She walked from one end of the cabin to the other, raising the phone high and dropping it low to see if she could find a connection. Nothing.

She shoved her phone back in her hoodie and looked around the room. Something was off. It took her a minute, but she realized what it was. She ran to the bedroom on the left side of the house and scanned the room before heading to the other side and scanning the second room.

No television. No radio. No Alexa. No computer. There were no electronics in the cabin anywhere. Nothing.

Well, what the hell did Apollo expect them to do instead? Her cheeks heated at memories of his hard, naked body.

Nope. They were *not* doing that. She'd not even done that with Ares… not really.

The breeze blew through an open window, and the scent of the woods called to her. Her wolf whined, wanting to be let free.

Well… just because she wouldn't fall for Ares didn't mean she couldn't run with him. It was only fitting that she be polite.

Her wolf howled, and River sighed before unzipping her hoodie and dropping it to the floor.

RIVER REVELED IN THE FRESH AIR THAT TRICKLED OVER HER SKIN AS she sprinted through the forest. It'd been too long since she'd been able to run. Much too long.

The city wasn't a great place to be a wolf. And she'd been too busy to drive out to the pack to run with them. Not that Cherry would have ever let her. So the feel of the dirt under her paws and the crunch of the leaves left her feeling rejuvenated and free.

It hadn't taken long for her to find Apollo. He'd not gone far, and her wolf instinctively ran straight for him. In her wolf form, the pull of the mating bond dragged her closer to him than she wanted, but there was no stopping it. She'd unleashed her wolf, so she had to go with what her wolf wanted, and her wolf wanted to sniff, play, and run- and she wanted to do it with Apollo.

Slut.

It wasn't like she hadn't been allowed to feel the bond between River and Ares growing. Even so, the greedy beast wanted Apollo as well, and there was nothing River could do to stop her.

THEY SPENT HOURS RUNNING AND ROMPING, AND WHEN THE SUN began to set, he took her out to a cliff, and they watched it dip below the horizon. Through it all, he didn't push her, didn't try to dominate her, didn't ask for a single thing from her. He was simply a companion to be with.

As the stars brightened in the sky, they stretched under them and stared at the moon.

"I love it here," Apollo said.

She'd not heard his voice in hours and hadn't realized he'd shifted back into human form, so the noise startled her, making him chuckle. She made sure to keep her eyes trained on the sky.

"Come on. I want to talk to you."

She continued to stare at the sky, though her wolf wanted to take in his naked body again.

"I promise not to look at you. I will be a total gentleman. I will keep my eyes trained on the sky the whole time. Scout's honor."

She glanced at his face. Seriously?

He chuckled. "Okay, I wasn't a scout, but I am a gentleman. Sometimes. Not always, I must admit, but one thing I can tell you about myself is that when I give my word, I never break it. Never."

His eyes grew serious, and she knew he meant what he said.

Reluctantly, her wolf gave up control to River, and she shifted to human form.

"Ah, there she is."

She folded her arms over her chest. "I thought you said you wouldn't look."

"I'm not. I can smell you. You smell different in human form than you do in wolf form."

She'd never noticed that before, but he was right. He smelled different in wolf form than he did in human form. His wolf form smelled... wilder. She couldn't explain it.

"Aren't the stars beautiful?"

She sighed. "I miss seeing them when I'm in the city. I grew up in a place like this and used to love lying under the stars."

"Me too."

She glanced over at him, and he smiled.

"Maybe I should make you promise not to look at me," he teased.

Her cheeks heated. "I... I'm... making sure you aren't looking at me."

He lay silent for a moment. "River, I don't know what my brother told you about me, but I promise I will never lie to you, and I will never go back on my word."

"Nothing," she said.

"What?"

"You said you didn't know what Ares said about you, and the answer is nothing. Until I met you today, I didn't even know you existed."

He snorted. "Doesn't surprise me. He's always been like that."

River's wolf bristled. She didn't like Apollo talking bad about Ares.

"You do know that talking badly about Ares won't win you any points with me or my wolf, right?"

"Oh, Kitten, trust me, I have plenty I could tell you if I wanted to turn you against him. What I said was simply the truth."

Pet names? Already? "Kitten?"

"Oh, you don't like that one. Okay, how about Sweetheart?"

"Meh."

"Meh? Well, we don't want you to have a *meh* pet name. How about Pookie?"

"No, thank you."

He chuckled. "Hunny Bunny?"

"Next."

"Lover Muffin?"

She didn't even bother to answer that one.

"How about, Princess?"

She snorted. "That one is new."

"What do you mean?"

She blew out a breath and sat up, wrapping her arms around her legs. "Let's just say I've always been more ride-or-die bitch than fairytale princess."

"Well, my fairytale princess would definitely be a ride-or-die girl, so it's perfect."

"Except everyone calls me that now."

Apollo shook his head. "No good. Kitten, it is."

River laughed and looked over at him. His eyes turned black. He sat up so fast that she flinched.

Apollo's fangs lengthened, and he growled. "He bit you."

"What?"

Apollo raised a tentative hand and touched her shoulder. Goosebumps rose on her skin, and her wolf howled.

River slapped her hand over the spot he stared at.

"My brother bit you. Marked you," Apollo accused.

"Yes… I mean, no."

"Yes or no?" His muscles twitched, and his voice held a threatening tone.

"Yes, I was bitten by your brother, but not Ares."

"What does that mean?"

"I guess he's your half-brother?"

"Titan bit you?" The rage in his voice cut right through her.

"About four years ago. He found me in my pack and attacked me."

"He claimed you? Without your permission?"

She didn't want to go into it again. River sighed. "Short story. He attacked me. I stabbed him a bunch of times with a potato peeler. I rejected him. My mom shot him. My Alpha kicked him out. I moved to the city and went to art school."

Apollo stared at her neck. "I'll rip his heart out with my bare hands."

She nodded. "That's pretty much what Ares said after we were attacked in New York."

"You and Ares were attacked by Titan in New York as well?"

How could twin brothers who disliked each other immensely have the same hair-trigger temper?

"Yes. Titan had apparently been watching me the whole time without my knowing. A bunch of rogues attacked. I'm not sure. Ares said it was me, but they didn't come after me. They attacked Ares and the others. All Titan did was scratch me."

"He hurt you?"

"Just a scratch. It was weird, though. We'd been in a crowd walking down some stairs, and he just… scratched me. I didn't even realize it was him until a moment later. My wolf told me it was him. I'm not sure why I didn't smell him beforehand. Maybe it was all the people. She decided to redirect the conversation. "It was in the opera house. We'd just finished watching Carmen."

Apollo stared at her for a long, tense moment, and then his posture relaxed a fraction. "I would have let them kill me if I'd been forced to sit through an opera."

River couldn't help but chuckle. "I liked it."

Apollo shook his head, and his eyes morphed back to hazel. "No thanks. Ares can have all his fancy prissy theater stuff."

"And where would you rather go?"

He shrugged. “Riding my bike. Camping. Hunting. The occasional concert or monster truck rally."

She nodded. "I like riding too. Not as much as I enjoy running, of course, but since I didn't get to run until about four years ago…"

"You never ran before four years ago?"

She shook her head. "I didn't find out I was an Omega until Titan bit me."

Apollo's brow furrowed. "How is that even possible?”

She sighed.

Apollo watched her for a moment, then lay back down and stared at the sky. "It's okay. You don't have to tell me everything right now. We have time. Lots of time."

River looked out at the stars. Time. Time with Apollo… Her wolf was conflicted. She wanted to spend time with Apollo. But she also wished she could return to the estate and be with Ares. His imposing, protective personality spoke to her like a match spoke to gasoline.

"Your turn."

River glanced at him and, upon seeing his nakedness, looked back at the sky again. "What do you mean?"

"What is your pet name for me going to be?" A rueful smile crept over his lips.

Many nicknames came to mind. Scoundrel. Rake. Cad. She was pretty sure he wouldn't like any of them.

"How about Mate?" he offered.

"Uh…"

He chuckled again. "Too soon? That's okay, Kitten, you think about it."

It amazed her that their tempers seemed to be the only thing they had in common. Ares had been demanding and overbearing, forcing his way into her life and commanding her heart. In the end, it worked, but… Apollo's easy air made her relax, like she could be herself.

She yawned, and her eyes fluttered shut.

"It's been a long day. Why don't I get you back so you can rest?"

She breathed deeply and curled onto her side into the earth. "Can't we sleep out here?"

"You'd want to do that? Won't you get cold?"

"I'll shift." She instantly did so.

"You're serious."

She blew out a breath and allowed the sounds of the forest to invade her. The crickets chirped, and in the distance, an owl hooted. Memories flooded her of sleeping out in the woods at Bianca's side with the pack or even alone. She'd not realized how much she'd missed it while living in the city until that moment.

A soft hand stroked down her body. "You sleep, Kitten. I'll make sure that nothing disturbs you."

APOLLO

APOLLO LAY STILL, WATCHING THE RISE AND FALL OF HER SILVERY body with each breath. Beautiful. Absolutely beautiful.

Apollo's wolf whined and paced, wanting to be released to be closer to her. To lay his head on hers and wrap himself around her and feel the heat of her body.

His heart went out to her, and a part of him felt guilty for pushing himself upon her, but he had no choice. Ares always took what he wanted, but not this time. This time, Apollo would fight. Fight for her. Fight for himself. Fight for the crown. He didn't care what it cost him. She would be his.

His thoughts turned to the mark on her neck. Titan. Damn, son of a bitch, Titan. Why hadn't Ares told him? Even if Ares didn't want him to have River, he should have told Apollo about the threat to River's safety. Just thinking of Titan attacking River, scaring her, biting her without permission, had his wolf ready to take down the world to burn Titan alive and eat his heart.

Titan had been a thorn in his and Ares' sides their entire lives. His mother hadn't been their father's fated mate. He'd been close to fifty when he'd finally found their mother. It'd been five years after he'd let the loneliness and fear of no legacy take his sense, and he'd chosen Titan's mother to bear him an heir. It had only taken a month for her to get pregnant. Ultimately, when their father found their mother, all hell broke loose with Titan's mom.

Apollo knew Titan hated them and wanted the crown for himself, but he never would have thought Titan would be so desperate as to try to claim an Omega without her consent.

He decided at that moment that no matter who River chose in

the end, he would do whatever it took to keep her safe from Titan. After all, whether she took him or Ares to mate, she would still be his Luna and Queen of the entire Lycan and shifter world. It would be his duty to protect her until the day he died.

CHAPTER FOUR

RIVER

The next morning, River and Apollo made their way back to the cabin, and she was surprised to see it fully stocked and a bodyguard she didn't recognize cooking breakfast. Apollo shifted and raced to another room before returning with a large blanket and wrapping her in it. Lachlan and the others turned away as she padded down the hall covered in the blanket. She shifted when Apollo closed a bedroom door behind them and grabbed the blanket to keep it from falling off her.

It surprised even her that she had shifted in Apollo's presence. Even though they'd been naked together under the moon, she had hidden herself with her hair and by curling up while in human form.

"You know I sprout fur when I'm a wolf, right? It's not like they are seeing me naked or something."

Apollo looked at her thoughtfully. "Until we are mated, no other male may see you in your wolf form."

"Really?" Another Lycan thing?

"Really."

"So you never run with your guards?"

"Occasionally."

"What about with your parents?"

"Obviously."

"So… what about my family? Can I run with them?"

"Of course."

"But no one else?"

"Yes."

She blew out a breath and sat on the bed, forcing herself to keep her eyes north of his chest, which wasn't easy when every instinct wanted to take in his beautiful naked form. Her body heated as she imagined running her hands over every taut inch of him.

Focus River! Keep your head out of the gutter!

She adjusted her blanket. "Is it just a Lycan thing that says I can't run with anyone else or…"

"You will be the High Luna of the world. You are the most sacred and revered female of our generation. That means you are to be protected and respected at all costs."

She wanted to ask him more questions, but noticed dark circles pooled beneath his eyes.

"Did you not sleep well?"

"I didn't sleep at all."

River's gut clenched. "I'm sorry. You should have told me you preferred to sleep in the cabin-"

"I don't. I love sleeping outside. But I told you I'd make sure you were safe."

Guilt raced over her. "Apollo. I'm-"

He knelt in front of her, pressing a finger to her lips. "Don't apologize. It was my choice and my pleasure."

The touch of his soft finger to her skin made her shiver, and her wolf howl.

Mine. My mate. My Alpha.

"Why don't you nap, and we can do something later?"

"Absolutely not. We only have a few days together, and I don't want to miss a moment."

River sighed and shook her head. As stubborn as his brother.

"Well, I'd like to take a shower."

Apollo nodded. "Of course. Let me just make sure that Silas got everything I asked for."

He opened the door, giving her a good look at his perfectly sculpted butt. He stepped out, and she cleared her throat.

Apollo looked back at her.

"Maybe... you need a blanket of your own?" She cocked an eyebrow at him.

Apollo chuckled. "My men and I have seen each other naked so many times we could name every freckle and scar on each other's bodies."

Apollo's comfort with being naked somehow suited him.

"My nakedness makes you uncomfortable."

"Not uncomfortable. It's just that since I wasn't raised like other shifters. I didn't go on runs with the pack or anything, and I'm not used to it."

He inclined his head. "Of course. I'm so sorry. I didn't realize."

"Besides, you don't want anyone seeing me when I'm naked."

Apollo growled.

"Well, do you think I like you walking around naked for everyone to see?"

His eyebrows scrunched together. "They're my men."

"Are they all mated? And not all men are into women. Even when it comes to shifters, did you ever think of that?"

He opened his mouth and then closed it again. He walked to the bed, pulled a blanket from the foot of it, and wrapped it around his hips.

"Thank you."

He winked at her. "Anything for you, Kitten."

Apollo closed the door, and River stared at it, replaying what she'd just said. Was she already putting a claim on Apollo? She'd pretty much done that by telling him she didn't want him naked with anyone else. Or was it just that she didn't like the one-sided way Ares and Apollo tried to hold her to rules that they didn't live by themselves?

Apollo's toned body entered her mind, and she heated. Damn, they were so hot. So hot. Both of them. And all they wanted was her. Her!

Her wolf chuffed and mewled.

"Shut up."

River plopped down on the bed. What was happening? How could she want two different men? She'd never even had one boyfriend before, let alone two.

How could her wolf want two men? She couldn't explain it. Her wolf wasn't ready to give her whole heart to one of them. And she couldn't give half a heart to both of them. Somehow, her wolf wanted to give herself wholly to both of them. Was that even possible?

The door opened, and Apollo stepped in. "I started the water for you. It's well water and can sometimes take a while to warm up. There are towels and other essentials in the bathroom for your use. If you are missing anything, we can get it while we're out today."

"Are we going somewhere?"

"I thought we might ride into town and look around a bit."

She nodded. "Sounds fun. Are you going to shower?"

"Is that an invitation?" Her cheeks heated, and he chuckled. "I love making you blush. You're adorable."

Adorable? That was a new one.

"I'm going to shower in a different cabin. Then we can eat and go to town."

"Sounds good. Before we go, can you do me a favor, though?"

"Anything."

"Could you introduce me to everyone living with us for the next few days? It'll be weird to call them all 'Bodyguard' or 'Hey You'. I get that you know them, but aside from Lachlan, I haven't spent more than a few minutes just seeing any of them."

"Well, that won't do. If you are to be my queen, you need to get to know my men even better than you know Ares'. I'll introduce you over breakfast."

Apollo gave a slight bow and left.

Her chest squeezed as she realized choosing between them was more significant than just picking a mate. Given their different personalities, their leadership styles would also be different. Whichever of them took the crown would determine the next reign of the werewolf nation. And it was up to her to pick who that would be.

Sheesh. No pressure or anything.

River closed her eyes and took several deep breaths. Why her? Why had it been put on her to choose? At that moment, she wished more than anything that she'd never found out she was an Omega.

After the shower, River changed back into her clothes from the day before and sat with Apollo and the bodyguards to eat. The chat easy and relaxed, like old friends. The air so different from the intensity of Ares and his men. She listened as they talked about old memories from being in the woods and things they'd done as kids.

"So, how long have you all known each other?"

"Bennet, I've known my whole life. His dad was my father's guard. Silas and I went to school together," said Apollo. "Since what? Third grade?"

"Second, I think," Silas replied.

Apollo smiled. "Yeah, second. The year we had Miss Tanson."

Bennett sighed, and a large, goofy smile planted on his freckled face. "Miss Tanson. I didn't even know what a crush was in second grade, but man, I had one hard for Miss Tanson."

"No shit." Silas snorted. "You knocked out my front tooth for saying I would marry her one day."

The men burst into laughter.

"What about you two?" she asked the men further down.

"Regan and Thomas, I found in college. We pledged the same fraternity."

"Where did you go to school?"

Suddenly, the table erupted into a football game rally as the group belted out their alma mater's school song.

The group broke into wild laughter, and River felt like she was at a pep rally.

"What did you study?"

"I have an MBA. I mostly handle the finances and business side of our empire."

"There's a business side to being a Prince?"

Apollo chuckled. "We have many investment interests and real estate holdings. We also own some companies and offer financing to Lycan and shifter business owners."

"So you work a nine-to-five job?"

"More like a five to two job. I get up early when the stock market opens and work mostly with companies on the East Coast, so I usually finish by noon or two p.m. It frees up my evenings. I like it that way."

She nodded, wondering who would take on his duties while he was away. Ares had enough on his plate without having to deal with the stuff Apollo handled.

She pushed her food around her plate as the men laughed and joked for several minutes.

River noticed Lachlan eating silently. "What about you? Did you grow up around here, Lachlan?"

He looked up from his plate and glanced around the table. "No, Highness. I'm from the Midwest."

"Where?"

"Oklahoma, Highness."

River shoveled a forkful of eggs into her mouth. "Do you miss it?"

Lachlan glanced around again. "Sometimes, Highness. I love the woods and trees here, but I do miss the open fields."

"If you aren't comfortable here, you are welcome to return to the estate," said Apollo.

River shot him a look.

He shrugged. "I'm just-"

"You are just trying to assert your dominance and make Lachlan feel uncomfortable, and that's not okay. He is here at my request. He didn't ask to be here. Hell, I bet he didn't even ask to become Ares' bodyguard. I understand that you may not have chosen him, but I did, and I expect you to respect that at the very least." His jab surprised her. She would have expected something like that from Ares, but Apollo? Obviously, she still had a lot to learn about him.

She refused to break eye contact with Apollo.

He inclined his head. "You are right, River. I apologize."

"To who? Me?"

Apollo looked between her and Lachlan. "To you both."

Lachlan bowed his head. "There is nothing to apologize for, Highness."

River growled. The male egos and kowtowing to those of a higher station were things she had never understood and never would get used to, not to others and especially never to herself. It was one thing she would insist on discussing with both Ares and Apollo when she got a private moment.

River set her fork down and rose from her seat. The others rose as well.

"Are you finished?" asked Apollo.

"I... I need some air." River strode around the table and to the front door.

Footsteps followed her, and she held up her hands. "I'm just going out the door. I don't need an entourage. If you need to, you can watch me from the window. But if one of you steps out that door, you are liable to get a boot to the balls or my knife somewhere equally as unpleasant."

She pulled open the door and walked out before any of them could reply. She stormed down the steps onto the dirt and gravel path and looked at the sun. She crossed her arms over her chest and closed her eyes. A minute passed, then another, before the tears started.

What had she gotten herself into? Politics? In fighting? Royalty?

Responsibility? She'd never asked for any of that. Never wanted any of it. Men following her. People not able to use her name. What next? Would she be forced to have all the elders watch her consummate her mating or watch her deliver her first child?

Maybe Alaska wasn't such a bad idea after all.

Soft footsteps crunched up behind her. She grabbed a knife from her boot, turned, and threw it. Apollo caught it midair.

The door burst open, and the men rushed out.

River grabbed her second knife.

Apollo spun around and lobbed her knife at one of the pillars on the porch, inches from Bennett's head. "If any one of you dares to lay a hand on my mate, I will kill you myself. I don't care if she stabs me with a poisoned dagger. You don't touch her. Ever. Are we clear?"

The men looked at each other and then bowed.

"Back inside," Apollo ordered.

River slid her second knife back into its holster and waited until the front door closed again before she swiped the tears from her eyes.

Apollo turned back to her. "I'm sorry, Kitten. I am truly sorry for upsetting you."

River waved him off.

He closed the distance between them and reached for her, but dropped his hand. "What is it? Tell me."

She shook her head. "Forget it."

He pressed his palm into her cheek, and she looked up at him.

"Tell me, River." His voice held tenderness.

"It's... everything. Leaving my home. Being an Omega. Being chased by Titan. Being bound to you and Ares. Having to choose between you. Having to choose at all. Knowing that my choice will determine the fate of the next reign of Lycan and shifter society. Just… all of it. I never asked for this. Never wanted this. I don't want this. I don't want this to be my choice. I don't-"

"Okay. Okay." Apollo wrapped her in his arms.

River laid her head on his chest, and the tears started again. And once they started, she couldn't stop them. It all came out. Everything she'd held back. Like a dam exploding after being overfilled. A lifetime of being lied to. The death of her father. Being forced to take pills and spray with sprays. Never being able to reach her wolf or run with the pack. Being attacked by Titan. The loneliness. The hiding. Never fitting in anywhere. Ares finding her. The attack at the theater. Moving to Canada. Being swept to a cabin in the middle of nowhere by a man she barely knew. Surrounded by other men she didn't know… All of it.

Apollo held her close, and after a minute, her body relaxed. She wrapped her arms around his waist and hung on to him.

He stood silently, holding her and letting her cry. Then, a soft rumble started in his chest and grew to a comforting hum. The vibrations soothed her soul, and soon, her tears dried. She let the low purr reverberate through her body, calming her.

Every worry vanished in one large exhale, and all she felt was peace. Suddenly, none of it mattered. Nothing mattered- only her and Apollo. The rest of the world just melted away.

She didn't know how long Apollo held her, but in those moments, River couldn't imagine anywhere else in the world she would rather be than in his arms.

APOLLO

The pain that wracked Apollo for making her cry was unbearable. He hadn't meant to upset her. He knew his words to Lachlan had been petty, but Lachlan's presence was just a reminder, every second of every minute, that Ares had gotten to River first. And before Ares, Titan.

It wasn't Lachlan's fault. In honesty, Lachlan was the only one of Ares' men he liked. But just having him there was like having Ares' eyes constantly upon them.

The feeling, though, of having her in his arms made all of that fade away. Right there, holding her after so many years of loneliness, was as close to heaven as he could imagine. His wolf whined and paced, wanting to comfort her.

We are boy. We are.

Then, strangely, he started to hum… no, not hum… something different. Something that didn't come from his vocal cords. It came from somewhere deeper. The hum morphed into a rumbly purr that filled his entire body. He'd only heard the sound once. He'd accidentally walked in on his father consoling his mother, and his father had made the same sound.

A smile spread across his face as he lay his cheek on her head. She really was his mate.

"I'm sorry," she finally said. "I didn't mean to freak out."

"You don't need to apologize. I can't imagine how overwhelming this situation must be."

She nodded.

"Do you want to talk about it?"

She shook her head. "Maybe later."

He kissed her head. "As you wish, Kitten."

She snorted and laughed. "Like in the Princess Bride?"

"What?"

She looked up at him. "You know, Wesley says 'As you wish' to Buttercup, but he means I love you."

He stared at her for a moment. "Oh… uh… I mean-"

She chuckled and shook her head. "I'm kidding. Take that terrified look off your face."

He blinked several times, unsure of what to say. "I've never seen the movie," he blurted.

"Everyone saw that movie. I don't even watch movies much, and I've seen it."

"Not a romantic comedy guy."

Her eyes narrowed.

"What?"

She shrugged. "You just seem the romantic comedy type, is all."

He winked at her. "That's because you don't fully know me yet. But you will. So, do you still want to go to town, or would you rather just stay here and relax today? I can have the guys stay outside to give you some space."

She wiped her eyes and face and then stepped away from him. "Either way."

He nodded. "Let's go into town. I think you'll like it."

She smiled. "It's a date."

Apollo couldn't help but return the smile. A date. With his mate. Could there be anything better?

CHAPTER FIVE

RIVER

They walked down the leaf-strewn street, and the laidback vibe calmed River's nerves. They walked into a general store.

"This place is adorable." She walked to an old teddy bear and picked it up. "I feel like I've walked into a fifties movie."

"This store is one of my favorites."

"Why?"

He chewed his lip for a minute, grabbed her hand, and pulled her to a section of shelves stocked with old board games.

She looked at them and up at him. "You like games?"

"I love board games. Especially rare and hard-to-find games or old games. My mom used to play with me. My father was gone a lot for business, and she and I used to play games to pass the time if he didn't take me with him."

She realized neither Ares nor Apollo talked about their parents.

She scanned the games, recognizing a few names but knowing nothing about them.

"I've never played board games."

"Never?"

She shook her head. "My dad and I used to do other things together. When Bianca and her father, Strider, moved in, Bianca only talked about Barbies, clothes, makeup, music, and boys. I spent most of my time watching out for her and doing what she wanted, or working out in the shop my dad left me. I don't even think I ever saw a board game in my house."

"I have hundreds of them. Every time my mom found a new one, she bought it."

"And you still have them?"

"Every single one... well... there is one game I don't have. My favorite game. We used to play it all the time, but Ares once got mad that Mom spent so much time with me, so he set it on fire."

She could almost see a frustrated pre-teen Ares taking it from Apollo and throwing the pieces into a fireplace one by one in vengeance.

She took his hand and squeezed it. "What game?"

He chuckled. "You know... I don't even remember the name. It had a bunch of animals in it. Kind of like Wind in the Willows or Beatrix Potter, but I don't remember exactly. I just remember that it used to be my favorite game."

How sad. "Well, do you have a new favorite game?"

He looked down at her, and his cheeks flushed a bit.

"I won't laugh. I promise."

He eyed her dubiously for a moment and then shook his head.

"Tell me."

He squeezed his eyes shut and blew out a breath. "It's called Parcheesi. It's simple but fun."

She looked at the shelf and found a copy. "This one?"

He opened his eyes and looked at it. "Yeah."

"Let's get it."

"That's okay."

She looked at the game and then at him. "I want to try it."

He took the game from her and put it back on the shelf. "Okay. I'll show it to you."

She looked at the game. "Then shouldn't we get it?"

He smiled. "I already have two copies at the cabin and three more at home."

She chuckled and shook her head.

"What? I want to ensure I always have a complete copy."

She nodded. "And how many of those five copies are new and unopened?"

He shrugged. "Only two."

Her wolf chuffed, and River reached up on her toes and kissed his cheek. "You are adorable."

She dropped back to her feet and stopped, realizing what she'd done.

Apollo's gaze grew serious, and heat rolled off his body. He reached out and cupped her cheek.

Her stomach fluttered, and her wolf howled and begged for more.

Apollo leaned in, and with every inch closer he moved, the more conflicted she became. Her wolf and her heart craved the feel of his lips on hers. But her brain screamed that it was wrong. She would be cheating on Ares.

An inch from her face, River stepped back, bumped into the shelf, and sent a bottle hurdling downward.

Apollo grabbed the bottle before it hit the floor. His gaze stayed on hers, and then he straightened and put the bottle back on the shelf.

He licked his lips and gave her a tight smile. "They have a candy counter on the other side of the store and make their fudge from scratch. You have to try it."

Her eyes widened. "Candy. Did you say candy? And real fudge?"

He offered her his arm. She set down the teddy bear she still held and took it.

Her wolf grumbled.

Oh, shut it! Just because you are ready to throw yourself at him doesn't mean I am a tramp. Did you forget about Ares so quick?

Her wolf whined, but River didn't know who she whined for, Apollo or Ares.

APOLLO PICKED OUT ALMOST ALL OF THE CANDIES IN THE OLD-fashioned jars to take back to the cabin with him. He smiled like a child when the store owner handed over the haul.

"What do you want?"

River snorted. "And I thought I had a sweet tooth. I think there's enough in that bag for both of us."

Apollo pulled the bag to his chest. "This is mine, Kitten. None of this 'No, I don't want dessert' business, and then you eat half of mine. If you want candy, get some."

She tried to discern if he was joking. But when he flashed her his fangs, she knew he wasn't.

Okay, sharing candy was off the table. Fair enough.

River got a two-pound fudge sampler and assured Apollo that she was not interested in sharing either. Then she got a box of fudge for each man as an apology for losing it earlier. Apollo said she didn't have to, but she insisted. She contemplated getting one for Ares but thought better of it.

They hadn't even left the store before Apollo dug into his candy. River handed boxes to Bennett, Silas, and Lachlan, each of whom bowed and thanked her. She made them stop before people began to stare.

She gave her box to Lachlan, who promised to keep it safe.

"I'm pretty sure no one is going to try to mug you for a box of fudge, but if you could keep it from melting, that would be great."

"I don't know," said Bennett. "This fudge is worth mugging someone for."

"What about you?" said Silas. "You gonna trust me with your giant suitcase-sized bag of Halloween candy?"

Apollo looked at him. "Hell no."

Everyone laughed, and then Silas took Apollo's candy.

"Why don't you focus on your mate, not your sugar tooth today?"

"Why can't I do both?"

"Because candy makes you crazy," Silas and Bennett said together.

"You remember when we were twelve, and Jonas took your candy bag? I thought you were going to put him in the ER."

"Dude. I was twelve. I'd spent hours going house to house for that haul."

"Well, for the safety of your mate, who might accidentally try and sneak one from you, we are keeping it."

Apollo growled and shook his head.

The dynamic between Apollo and his men differed significantly from Ares and the others. Ares was cautious, serious.

Apollo grabbed a candy stick from his bag and shoved it in his mouth before taking her hand. "There's a place I want to show you down the street. Then we can stop at the little shop across the way and get you more clothes."

She nodded, and they headed down the sidewalk. She looked over her shoulder to see Silas digging into Apollo's bag of candy.

She suppressed a giggle. They'd better not try that with her fudge, or they'd lose a hand.

APOLLO

Apollo did everything he could to fight his inner beast. Her rejection of his kiss sent his wolf into overdrive, and it had taken every ounce of strength to keep the animal from emerging and ripping the store apart and marking her right there.

So he'd done the only thing he could think of; he'd distracted himself, and the only distraction was the candy counter. With each sugary delight he popped into his mouth, his wolf became diverted enough for Apollo to calm him. It was stupid, and he didn't understand it, but for some reason, if his animal couldn't screw or kill, only food calmed him. Especially desserts and sweets.

By the time they left the store, his wolf was calm enough to lie down. That didn't mean he wasn't still grumbling, though.

Mine. Mate. Omega.

Trust me, I get it. But that's not the way.

Mine. Take.

Ours. No take. She gives.

His wolf grumbled and then huffed.

For the moment, he had calmed the beast enough to keep him from escaping his tether, but Apollo wasn't sure how long he'd be able to keep that tether on lockdown.

"What did you want to show me?"

Apollo pointed to the shop at the end of the corner. "It's right there."

They walked the rest of the way in silence, and when they came to the shop, he watched her reaction.

A smile spread across her face, and her eyes sparkled when she looked at him. His wolf howled.

"Wood carving?"

"The man who makes them has been doing it for over forty years. The big ones he does with a chainsaw in the back."

"That is so cool." She pulled open the door, and he held it for her as she entered.

The scents of pine, cedar, redwood, and more permeated the store, along with varnish and motor oil.

A bell tinkled overhead, and River headed straight to a giant statue of a bear standing in the corner.

"Wow." She looked up at the eight-foot behemoth.

Apollo still had no idea how the older man did it, how he achieved such fantastic detail with such enormous tools.

River ran her fingers over the bear and then turned her attention to a statue of two smaller cubs.

"These are unbelievable."

"Thank you." An older man emerged from the back room.

River looked up at him. "You are so talented."

He chuckled, and his belly jiggled in his overalls. "All it takes is practice. Anyone could do it."

River shook her head. "You're being modest. I sculpt with metal, which you can do with practice, but this…" She gestured around. "This takes talent."

The gentleman waved her off. "You could do it too if you tried."

"Me?"

"Why not?"

An idea popped into Apollo's head. "Would you be willing to give her a lesson? I'd pay, of course."

The man looked at him and shrugged. "Sure. You don't need to pay me, though. Just seeing her beautiful face is payment enough."

Apollo's wolf raised his head and growled. Apollo pulled out his wallet. "I insist."

He handed three hundred-dollar bills to the man.

The man shrugged and pocketed the cash. He held out his hand to River.

"I'm Walt."

"River. And this is my…" She looked at Apollo. "This is Apollo."

Apollo shook the man's hand, taking stock of his firm grip.

"Well, come on," said Walt. "I just put a couple pieces of fresh wood out back."

"Now?"

Apollo shrugged. "Unless you want to wait."

She shook her head vigorously, and Apollo smiled at making her happy.

"How about I get us some coffee from across the street and come back and join you?"

"Strong and black," said Walt. "Denise knows how I like it."

Apollo nodded and looked at River.

"Just a large soda, please."

"What kind?"

"Surprise me." She smiled at him and then followed Walt into the backroom. The two began to chat as they went, and Apollo's wolf grumbled.

"Oh, please, he's old enough to be her grandfather."

Mine.

"Fine. If he touches her, I'll let you eat him. Happy?"

His wolf wasn't happy. Not one bit. And if Apollo was being honest, he wasn't either, but he knew one thing for sure- if he wanted to win over River, he needed to be patient. Patient and calm. The two characteristics his twin did not possess.

CHAPTER SIX

RIVER

River spent four hours with Walt having him teach her how to wield the chainsaw to make the precise cuts needed for her design. She couldn't stop the joy that learning a new art form gave her.

To her surprise, she picked it up fast, and under Walt's tutelage, she was quite proud of how her sculpture was turning out.

For the entire four hours, Apollo watched her work. He drank his coffee, made a couple of phone calls, and talked to Silas for about five minutes at one point, but other than that, his eyes remained on her. The idea that Apollo had seen what she loved to do and had allowed her to do it turned her on.

But the longer he watched her, the more agitated her wolf became. She didn't just want Apollo's gaze on her. She wanted other parts of him as well. Strangely enough, River found herself doing things she'd never done before. She flirted with Apollo.

First, she'd taken off her shirt, tripping to her cami, exposing her arms and upper chest to him. Then she'd put her hair up, exposing her neck and throat. Finally, she'd made an effort to bend over in front of him to give him a perfect picture of her rear end.

After bending over, she'd stood to find him directly behind her. He pressed his body into hers. Her flirting worked. His lips fell close to her ear, and his warm breath tickled her neck.

"I think it's time we get back to the cabin."

He slid an arm around her waist, and she laced her fingers into his. "Could we do one more thing first?"

"I'm not sure I have the self-control for one more thing," he breathed, making her skin pebble.

"I want to go for a ride."

"In the car?"

She looked at him. "On your bike."

A smile crept across his face, and he kissed her forehead. "Kitten, how do you speak my language so well?"

She gripped his large hand. "How do you speak mine?"

They stared at each other for a heated moment, and River's wolf begged her to kiss him.

"I'll tell Silas to bring my bike. You finish up here." He squeezed her hip and then walked into Walt's store.

River watched him go, remembering what his tight, round rear looked like without being covered by his jeans. She wanted nothing more than to squeeze that rear as he settled between her thighs and made love to her.

"You two make a cute couple," Walt broke through her thoughts.

River whirled around and gave a nervous laugh.

"Even an old codger like me can see when two people are meant to be together. The way he looks at you... I used to look at my wife like that."

"I'm so sorry. Did she pass?"

Walt chuckled. "Nope. Left me for a trucker about fifteen years ago. Maybe it's because I stopped looking at her like that."

River wasn't sure what to say. "Thank you for teaching me, Walt. I really appreciate it."

"You are welcome to come back and finish anytime."

She nodded. "I have a few more days here. I would love to. Of course, I will pay you for the wood and your time."

"There's no need. It's a joy seeing someone love it as much as I do. Besides, when you weren't looking, your date slipped me another handful of bills."

Walt put on his goggles and started his chainsaw again, returning to his log.

River walked through the back room to his store, then out front. She looked down the street and saw Apollo talking to Silas and the others. Lachlan looked her way and gave her a small wave before getting in the car with Silas and Bennett.

River sucked in a deep breath and looked around. Small shops dotted the main road, much like an old town she might see in a movie. A hardware store. A quilting store. An antique store. A real estate office. A bar. A diner. A beauty salon. Everything people could need without the feel of big business taking over. Surprisingly, she found herself thinking about how nice it might be to live such a life. In the woods. Working on her art. Simple. Calm. If she ended up with Apollo, she wondered if that might be possible.

She smiled. A scent hit her, and she looked around. Across the street, a man stared at her in front of a hardware store. The hairs raised on her arms, and a sudden chill blew over her. Grabbing her shirt from around her waist, she pulled it over her head, covering herself. The man didn't move.

River's wolf growled, and River sniffed the air again. The man didn't smell like a shifter, but that didn't make her any less uneasy.

"Hey-"

River jumped and struck out at the newcomer.

Apollo grabbed her fist, amused for a second, but then his smile dropped. "What happened?"

She shook her head and looked across the street. The man was gone.

Apollo gripped her shoulders. "River?"

"It... It's nothing," she said, trying to calm herself. "There was a man across the street, staring at me."

"A shifter?"

"I'm sure it's because I stood here in my cami, but still... With everything that's happened, it creeped me out."

"Of course it did." Apollo scanned the street. "Go into Walt's and wait. I'll be back in a minute."

"Apollo-"

His gaze hardened, and he looked more like Ares than ever. "Inside, Kitten. I'll be right back."

His Alpha aura washed over her, and she knew better than to argue. He wasn't ordering her, yet her wolf was eager to comply.

She nodded and walked back into Walt's shop. Apollo took off across the street.

He sniffed the air, turned left, and tore down the sidewalk. She hugged herself, and her wolf paced. She wished Ares were there. River reached into her pocket and pulled out her phone. She had only 8% battery but two bars.

She went to her contacts, and her finger hovered over Ares' name. More than anything, she wanted to hear his voice.

She stopped.

If she called him, he would freak out and come to find her, but she didn't want that. Did she?

No. She didn't want to cause any further rift between the brothers. For the first time, she wondered if the twin she didn't choose would leave the estate. If she would never see them again. The idea made her gut twist. How would she possibly live without one of them?

The bell rang over the door, and River shoved her phone in her pocket.

"Hey. It's okay. I found the guy."

"Did you hurt him?" she blurted.

Apollo chuckled. "He was a human. A drunk human. But a human. If he'd been a shifter or a threat, I would have ripped his eyes out and fed them to him for looking at you and scaring you. Luckily, he wasn't."

River chuckled. "You're kidding, right?"

Apollo's grin spread across his face, and his eyes darkened. "Absolutely."

Her gut clenched. He wasn't kidding at all. River realized that, as different as Apollo and Ares might be, they were the same in their desire and protection of her.

APOLLO

TEN MINUTES LATER, SILAS RETURNED WITH APOLLO'S BIKE, followed by Bennett in the car. They left Walt's store, and as River put on her helmet, Apollo talked to Silas.

"Do a sweep of the town."

"Did something happen?"

"I just want to be... cautious."

Silas's gaze flicked to River and then back to Apollo. "Of course."

"Oh, and Silas. Wait until we are out of sight before getting the drunk man in the alley to a hospital. I don't want River to see."

Silas sniffed the air. "Will do."

"We'll be back in a couple of hours. I'm taking her to the point."

Silas nodded.

Apollo hopped on the bike, and River slid behind him as he put on his helmet. This time, she didn't hesitate to wrap her body around his and hug him tight. The thought made Apollo smile.

He glanced over his shoulder to the alley where he'd left Chad, the drunk human, before pulling away from the curb. He'd hurt Chad, but nothing permanent. He'd suggested somewhat physically that Chad not stare at women on the street. Chad had promised he wouldn't. Then Apollo suggested that Chad see a doctor to have his nose examined so it wouldn't heal crooked.

THEY'D TRAVELED FOR NEARLY FIFTEEN MINUTES ON THE HIGHWAY when River relaxed into him. She laid her head on his back and swirled her fingers over his belly. Her touch made his wolf chuff.

Easy boy. We still have a long way to go.

His wolf grumbled and then turned his attention back to River. They rode another twenty minutes, and Apollo pulled off the road onto a small dirt path. It'd been years since he'd been down the road, but he still knew every inch of it. He slowed the bike as they neared the clearing that led to the cliff's edge overlooking a canyon.

Ten feet from the edge, he stopped and cut the engine. He pulled off his helmet, took his and River's, and set them on the bike. Taking her hand, he pulled her closer to the edge. About five feet away, she stopped moving.

"Uh… I don't do heights," she confessed.

He pulled her chin so she looked at him, not at the edge. "I won't let anything happen to you."

Her eyes held uncertainty, but she nodded anyway.

He pulled her a few feet closer, and when he caught the scent of her fear, he stopped, and they sat.

Her hand stayed firmly clamped in his for several minutes before she relaxed. He could still hear the rapid beat of her heart, but she'd stopped sweating, and her fear diminished.

"It's beautiful."

Apollo nodded. "It's the best view of the canyon."

"How did you find it?"

"I used to come up to the cabins with my family when I was young. Back then, there were a lot of cousins and extended family who used the cabins when they got married or gave birth. They all sort of stopped, though, after my parents died. But when we came, I would explore everything I could, and one day, I stumbled onto this spot." He laughed. "My mom was so mad. I didn't realize how long I'd been gone, and we had to get my father to the airport. She was frantic when she found me. I wasn't quite sure if she'd hug me to death for not being dead or kill me for being alive."

River smiled. "I've been there. Though I'm pretty sure I was closer to death with my mom than you ever would have been with yours."

"Your mom's tough, huh?"

"The toughest. She's our pack enforcer for a reason. I've never met anyone who didn't back down from my mom except Ares. Even our pack Alpha gives in to her on occasion."

"Wow. Is she an Omega?"

"Nope. Just one stubborn bitch."

"I think I'd like her."

River snorted. "Don't say that until you've met her. Maybe it's better if you don't meet her until after we are mated."

River stopped abruptly, and her gaze met his.

"I… I mean, if we are mated," she said softly.

Apollo's emotions went from ecstatic to deflated in two seconds. He pushed a smile onto his face anyway and fought for something to say.

"Thank you for today," said River. "I can't tell you how amazing it was, and the fact that you let me do it and just sat and watched… it was unbelievable."

"Well, you did give me a good show. It was hard to tear my eyes away."

She blushed and pushed her hair back. "Yeah… uh… I've never done that before."

"You mean a strip tease pole dance while holding a chainsaw?"

She snorted. "Flirt."

He smiled. "You were flirting with me?"

She shrugged.

His wolf howled.

"Don't look at me like that. You're making it weird." She let her long hair fall over her face, covering it.

"I am? I'm sorry. Here, how about this?"

Apollo reached over, brushed the hair from her face, and kissed her. The sensation of his lips brushing against hers made his wolf jump around like a rabbit in a frying pan.

He only let a soft kiss last a moment before breaking away. "Your flirting worked."

River's eyes flooded with emotion, and then her scent grew spicy. She leaned in and pressed her lips to his, and for a moment, he could do nothing more than breathe at the prospect that she was kissing him. But soon, his wolf caught up with him, and Apollo gripped her by the hair at the base of her neck and deepened the kiss. Her taste exploded on his tongue like an ice cream sundae.

River mewled like a kitten, and Apollo couldn't hold back the hungry growl that emanated from him.

He wanted her. Goddess knew he wanted her. There on the ground. In the forest. Naked and beautiful and his.

He pressed River back with his body and covered her petite frame with his. Lying against her, his wolf flew into overdrive.

Mate. Omega. Mine. Take her. Bite her.

Apollo pushed his wolf's thoughts from his head. He settled his hips on hers and reveled in the curvy softness of her body.

Apollo kissed down the side of her neck, tasting every centimeter of her skin. He wanted to know everything about her. Every inch. Every dimple. Every curve. Everything. He wanted to memorize her with his mouth as well as every other part of his body.

He kissed down over her shirt to her belly and lifted the hem so he could swirl his tongue on her skin.

River bucked against him and raked her fingers through his hair. The stimulation to his scalp made him go hard in his jeans.

Apollo took his time rolling his tongue over her abdomen, and then a thought stopped him dead.

Had she slept with Ares?

"What?" She looked down at him.

Shit! He said that out loud.

"Uh…" He swallowed, willing himself not to ask. Thoughts of Ares having River pinned against the wall. In a luxury bed in that stupid penthouse hotel room. In the hot tub on the roof bombarded him.

"Did you have sex with Ares?" he finally asked.

River stared at him, and her eyes widened.

"I understand if you did, but I just need to know. Have you been with him already?"

River's features morphed, and her eyes flashed. She pushed Apollo off and sat up.

"I am here, with you, kissing you, and you want to know what Ares and I did?"

Guilt made his wolf's tail droop. "I'm sorry. I shouldn't have asked, but-"

"But what?" Her eyes flashed a beautiful Omega gold, and the stare she gave him would have withered lesser Lycans.

Apollo sighed and looked out over the canyon. Thoughts jumbled as he fought for the right words.

"River, did you feel it when we first met? When you touched me for the first time in the hallway right before Ares, and I got into a fight? Did you feel like you'd found your other half, your missing piece?"

River chewed the inside of her cheek. "Yeah."

"Well, that's how I feel every minute since I've met you. My head, my heart, and my wolf want nothing else besides you. But for you, you feel that for more than just me. You feel it for the one person I loathe most next to Titan. And that drives me to the brink of needing to kill him. Not wanting to kill him, actually needing it. You have no idea how hard it is to hold back. To not bite you. To not make love to you. To not... Look, I'm not trying to make you feel bad or pity me or any of that manipulative shit. I want you to know how hard it is for me as a Lycan, an Alpha, and a mate not to have already made you mine. And I just need to know. I need to know if you have slept with Ares. It won't change how I feel about you. I don't think anything could do that, but I need you to tell me the truth."

River looked at him with determination set on her face. "You think this is easy for me? I want those things, too, but I'm torn. Torn in my head and my heart. I understand that you and your brother don't have a good relationship. But I will not be a pawn in either yours or his pissing match. What's between you two is between you. Not me. And if you want any kind of relationship with me, I suggest you refrain from asking stupid questions. Jealousy doesn't endear me. But to answer you, no. I have not slept with Ares."

Relief flooded Apollo. At least Ares hadn't beaten him to that.

He reached for her, but River stood. "I'd like to go back to the cabin now."

Apollo dropped his hand. "Of course."

They walked back to the bike, and Apollo handed her a helmet. She reached to take it, but when he hung on to it, she looked at him.

"I'm sorry for ruining our moment together."

She scowled. "Me too."

CHAPTER SEVEN

RIVER

River tossed and turned most of the night. After Apollo's question she needed some space. Not that she got any. There was the inside and the outside of the cabin, and that was about it. Despite being surrounded by woods, she couldn't have been alone if she'd tried. Apollo would have been there every second, dogging her steps and reminding her she'd kissed him and how conflicted that made her. She loved the feeling of his lips on hers but, at the same time, felt traitorous to Ares. She wondered if she would feel the same about being with Ares when she returned to the estate as she did about being with Apollo. If she didn't, did that mean she'd made her choice?

River sighed and sat up. Having locked herself in the room since returning, her skin itched to get out. She used to feel safe in confined spaces, but ever since her wolf's emergence, confined spaces only reminded her of the years of keeping her wolf in a cage. Never letting her out. Never letting her run free. And being so close to the woods only compounded the issue. Her wolf knew what lay beyond the wooden walls, and she wanted to go out and run through the trees.

River stood from the bed and looked at her phone to check the time before shaking her head and putting it on the nightstand again. Her phone had died the night before. She cursed herself for the dozenth time for forgetting a charging cord. She would've asked Lachlan if he had one, but she didn't want to get him in trouble with Apollo. He'd gotten an earful the night before just for entering River's room to bring her food. If it hadn't comforted her to have him there, she would have sent him back to the estate for his own good.

River picked up her clothes for the third day and smelled them. Yuck. She needed fresh clothes, so she wrapped herself in a blanket instead.

River opened her bedroom door and found Apollo sleeping on the floor. Hands behind his head, he wore only a pair of sweats. Her wolf howled at the sight of his toned body. Every muscle stacked on the last, and though he wasn't as wide as Ares, he was in no way smaller. She couldn't help the flush of heat that rushed through her body. Her wolf paced, agitated that she had not yet been able to mate with either of her two Alphas. River's mind wandered, and she thought about running her hand down Apollo's rigid torso. About his heated mouth on hers again. His hands on her body.

Okay, she needed to cool down.

Apollo opened his eyes. Heat flushed River's cheeks, but she didn't look away.

"Does that scent you are giving off mean you forgive me for being a jackass?"

"Why don't you come here and find out?"

She couldn't believe the words left her mouth, but as soon as they did, a small smile quirked up the corner of Apollo's mouth.

Like a prowling tiger staring down his prey, he got to his feet and stalked toward her. River backed up until she hit the wall. Apollo's eyes never left her face. He caged her inside his arms and leaned into her. But before his lips could touch hers, she stopped him.

"Are you really sorry?"

Apollo growled. "Eternally."

"Prove it."

Apollo's eyes went black, and he traced a finger down her throat. "How?"

She shrugged. "You're the Alpha of Alphas. I'm sure you can think of something."

Apollo looked down the hallway toward the living room, pulled her into her room, and shut the door, locking it- not that any of the other men would dare enter.

He picked her up and lay her on the bed, making her body pebble with desire. He stared at her for a long minute, knelt beside the bed, and pulled her towards him. River quaked with anticipation.

Delicately, Apollo unwrapped the blanket from her leg and, starting at her toes, kissed and nipped her skin, placing languid sucking kisses on her heel, her ankle, her calf. And with every kiss, her wolf grew needier.

River threw her head back and moaned as he worked his way up to the back of her knee and then unwrapped her thighs and kissed up the inside of her leg.

River trembled as he stopped at the top of her thigh and waited.

His hot breath fell onto her most sensitive places, making her nipples harden.

"Don't stop now," she panted.

He chuckled, and then, without warning, his mouth clamped down hard on her nub as his tongue flicked inside her.

River almost came apart right then. She grabbed Apollo's hair and bucked her hips into him. He wrapped his arms around her thighs and pulled her tight against his mouth.

River couldn't help the noises that emanated from her as he wound her higher and closer to the edge.

"Apollo," she gasped his name. "Apollo."

He bit the inside of her thigh hard and slid a finger inside her. It was over for her in that moment. She cried out, unable to stop herself. Wave after wave of pleasure wracked her as he continued to kiss and nip at her skin, rocking her through her climax.

When the spasms subsided, she fell back against the bed, spent. With a satisfied growl, Apollo continued to kiss a path up her body. Across her hip. The dip of her waist. The side of her ribs, where she promptly burst out laughing.

He looked up at her and smiled. "Ticklish?"

She shook her head. "Nope."

He cocked an eyebrow and then leaned in again and kissed her in the same spot.

River squealed and edged away from him, laughing. But her torso was tucked into the blanket, so she wasn't able to move freely, and he caught her by the arms and pressed her wrists over her head.

He looked down at her. "Hmmm... conundrum. If I let go of your hands, you'll wiggle away. But because I'm holding your hands, I can't uncover those beautiful breasts I've been dying to see."

She cocked an eyebrow. "Then do something else."

"Kitten, there are so many things I want to do. Trust me, I'm not at a loss for imagination."

River pressed her lips to his and plunged her tongue into his mouth. He growled and kissed her hard. Their teeth clashed, and tongues swirled together, as he claimed every part of her mouth until her lips were swollen and sensitive.

"River…" He could barely get her name out in a groan. "I want to make love to you."

Her heartbeat quickened, and she kissed him harder. Damn, she wanted to feel him inside her. Making love to her. Her wolf spurred her on, wanting him as well.

"River… tell me I can have you. Tell me to bite you and make you mine."

She gasped for breath. He was asking her permission. Not demanding. Not taking without consent. He was actually asking her. In that moment her heart flayed open, and she wanted nothing more than to tell him yes.

"I… I can't," she said without thinking. Dammit! "I want to, you have no idea how much I want you to, but I can't. You know I can't."

Apollo let out a shuddered breath and pressed his forehead to hers.

"I'm sorry," she whispered. "I am, Apollo. But-"

He kissed her forehead. "You don't need to explain. I wish it weren't this way, but I understand."

Pain squeezed River's chest, and a tear leaked from her eye. Apollo kissed the tear away and rolled off her, pulling her into his arms.

"Don't cry, Kitten."

"This is just… why? Why does it have to be like this?"

The purr started in Apollo's chest, and he pulled her closer, trying to soothe her. "It seems like the ultimate twist of fate in my life."

"I always wanted someone of my own. My own fated mate. But not this… not two I had to choose between. I…"

"Shhhh…" He kissed her head, and she wrapped her arms around him, letting his warmth and vibrations radiate through her like a soothing balm.

How? How did she choose when everything inside her told her she couldn't?

APOLLO

Apollo's wolf howled at the feel of River's pain. He wanted to be let out to comfort her.

Mine. My mate.

Yeah, bud. I know.

Mark. Take.

No, that's not what she needs.

His wolf grumbled.

Apollo's wolf wasn't the only part of him that wanted to take River and make her his. But he told his smaller head to chill out as well.

He'd never wanted or needed anything so much in his life as he did River, and yet he kept himself from taking that one thing. From claiming her and making her his forever. It went against everything he'd ever been taught. Every instinct. Every desire. It was like telling himself he didn't need to breathe anymore. It didn't matter how long he held his breath. Eventually, he would breathe again. And he knew it would be the same with River if he wasn't careful.

Sooner or later, his instincts would take over. He just prayed that when they did, he would also have the strength to hold himself back. Or, better yet, that she would say yes.

RIVER

"What should we do today?"

Apollo pulled her closer. "I like what we're doing right now."

Her stomach rumbled, and she laughed. "I do, too, but my stomach has other opinions."

"Then it's good I sent Bennett out this morning for a bakery run."

River shot up. "You mean you've had baked goods waiting and didn't tell me?"

He shrugged. "Why would I tell you when you taste better than any pastry ever could?" A roguish smile crossed his face.

She leaned in close and stopped just an inch from his mouth. "Because I didn't get to eat."

"You're welcome to taste any part of me."

River couldn't help but smile. He raised his hand to touch her face, but she jumped off the bed and made for the door.

She'd just gotten it open when Apollo leaped up and slammed it shut. A growl escaped him.

"There is no way in hell you are going out there in just that sheet."

She looked down. "But my clothes stink, and I have nothing else to wear."

He nodded. "I will go get you the food."

"I don't want to be cooped up here all day."

"Then I will send Bennett to get you some clothes."

"He won't know what I'd wear."

"Then tell me, and I will tell him."

They stared at each other for a long minute, and Apollo folded his arms over his chest and leaned back against the door.

"Unless you want me to rip the eyes out of my men as well as your darling Lachlan, I suggest you allow me to bring you the food."

River growled. "Ugh! Alphas!"

"Ugh! Omegas!" he teased.

River rolled her eyes. "Fine. T-shirts, jeans, leggings. Nothing formal."

Apollo nodded and opened the door.

"Oh, and I need underwear and a bra," River called. "Does he need to know my sizes?"

Apollo turned to her, his eyes black. "No other man will ever know your sizes but me from this day forward."

She couldn't help but laugh. "Then how do you know what he gets will fit me?"

"I'll make sure he gets you some nice, big, granny panties." Apollo winked at her.

River was about to tell him he better not dare when he closed the door.

Bennett better not return with granny panties because if he did,

Apollo would freak when she went commando instead of wearing them.

THE OUTER DOOR OPENED TEN MINUTES LATER, AND THE SMELL OF coffee and muffins hit her nose. Apollo slid into the room, and she moaned.

"I could eat everything in your hands."

Apollo smiled and handed her a tray of assorted pastries. Each looked better than the last, and she didn't know where to start.

Apollo set his cup of coffee on the nightstand, reached into his pocket, and pulled out a bottle of soda.

River smiled. "My hero!"

He chuckled. "If I'd known all it took to win you over was a bottle of soda, I would have brought an entire truck full."

She ripped off the top and took a long, burning drink. She sucked in a huge breath and then burped.

Apollo sat on the bed and touched her cheek. "So gentile."

She looked right at him and burped again.

He chuckled and shook his head. He reached for a Danish, and she swatted at his hand.

"I told you I could eat everything."

"Does that mean you aren't sharing?"

"Hmmmm... Maybe. If you answer a question for me."

"You can ask me anything."

She grabbed a muffin and picked at it, trying to figure out the best way to ask him the question that had been burning inside her for the last two days.

"Why do you and Ares not get along?"

Apollo sat silent for a moment and sipped his coffee. "Ever

since we were little, Ares just commanded attention. From our parents. From females. From everyone. I just didn't possess the same charisma he did. So, everyone gravitated to him. I saw it in people's eyes. Heard the whispers behind my back. They all wanted him to be the Alpha of Alphas. So I lashed out. When he got things he loved, I took them or destroyed them. Soon, it became clear that where people loved Ares, they feared me. And that was enough to keep me in the top position. But then… our parents died, and things just got worse. Where I thought our parents' deaths might bring us closer, it did the total opposite. People thought we would fight for the throne and started picking sides. The problem was, to be king, one of us needed a mate. So we've pretty much separated duties in an uneasy truce of sorts. Until now. I'm better at diplomacy, and he's better as the enforcer."

"Then why didn't you come to New York instead of him?"

"Because with the rogues on the rise, he convinced me that a more commanding presence would be needed there. He wasn't wrong. He got more Alphas to agree to join us than I probably could have. But it does make me sad that he found you and not me."

"I'm sorry. It seems all I've done is make things worse for both of you."

Apollo set down his coffee and took her face into his large palms. "You have brought me more joy in the last two days than I've known in my entire life. I would give up the throne, my brother, and everything else just to have you."

River swallowed hard. What the hell did she say to that? She wondered if Ares would be willing to do the same, but she already knew the answer.

"Your parents died in an accident, right?"

Apollo sat back on the pillows and blew out a sigh. "That's what we said, but no- Titan killed them."

River's gut clenched. How could one man cause so much pain?

"He ambushed them at their favorite restaurant. After poisoning them with silver, he killed them. It's why he went into hiding. It's been six years since we heard anything."

"Apollo... I'm so sorry. Losing my dad was terrible, but losing both parents at the same time... I can't imagine."

Apollo gave her a sad smile. "It hasn't been easy, that is for sure. I loved my parents dearly. They were generous and strong people. I hope I can be half the king my father was."

River wanted to reassure him that he would be, but, with the choice, she couldn't promise he would be the next king.

"I wish they could've met you. They would have loved you. Especially my mom."

She smiled. She could pretty much see her dad and Apollo bonding over a beer. Laughing, fishing, hanging out. But he would also appreciate Ares' strength. He'd have felt comforted knowing that River had ended up with a mate who could protect and provide for her. But if her father were still alive, would Titan have ever even found her? They'd never have moved to the new pack, and maybe she never would have even met the twins.

"Where has Titan been? I know he's been watching me in New York. Do you think he could have been there all this time?"

Apollo shook his head. "No idea. And that's a good thing because if I knew where he was, I'd freaking kill him for what he did to you and my parents."

The anger that flashed in his eyes made him look like Ares had at the opera house.

Her stomach plummeted. She couldn't see him doing anything

like that. Ares, absolutely, but Apollo was too… gentle, considerate, kind. He wasn't a killer.

"Anyway." He broke the silence. "Tell me about your childhood."

She sipped her soda and then picked up a cinnamon roll. Pulling a piece off, she stuck it into her mouth.

"My dad died when I was nine. My mom had been the enforcer for years before it happened. She'd never been very maternal to begin with, but after my dad died, something inside her died, too. She became the ultimate weapon. Unhinged weapon, but still a weapon."

"And your dad, what did he do?"

"Took care of me."

"That's different."

"True. He was an Alpha, but in many ways, he was like you. Laid back, funny, kind. That's why he didn't want to become a pack leader. He was afraid that if he became one, he'd be forced to do things he didn't want to do. My mom's uptight and on edge enough for both of them." River snorted.

"Who looked after you after he died?"

"No one. I mean, Strider and Bianca moved in a few days after he died. Strider's wife died in a car accident a few years prior. So he and Bianca moved to try to get a new start. Strider and Mom knew each other when they were younger, I think. She doesn't talk about it. Anyway, they got together, and I had a little sister I needed to look out for suddenly."

"I heard something about your sister being mated to one of Ares' men?"

"Yup. Zeke."

"One of the new ones."

River shrugged. "I don't know how long he's been with Ares."

"So, she's your sister?"

"Pretty much. Mom and Strider have never mated, but they've been together for fifteen years."

"Interesting."

"Haven't there ever been Lycans that have been together but not mated?"

He shook his head. "We're too possessive."

"Lycans really are different from shifters."

His brow creased. "Are we? I can't imagine any male not feeling the same."

She couldn't argue with that. Maybe her mom had resisted mating Strider all these years. River wouldn't put it past her.

"So, did your dad mate Titan's mom?" She picked another piece of cinnamon roll.

Apollo stared at his coffee cup.

"I'm sorry, it's none of my business."

"No, it is your business. You, of anyone, should know the truth. He never mated or married Titan's mom. I think that angered Titan most. The way Dad just threw her aside so easily. Not that it would have mattered even if he'd mated her. In the past few days, I've learned I would give up anything or anyone just to be with you."

"What about his brother Osmodius? Osmodius could have carried on the bloodline."

"Osmodius is my mother's brother, not my father's. Her twin brother, actually."

"Oh." River wondered what Titan and Titan's mother had endured after his father had found his fated mate. She couldn't even imagine. For a split second, she felt terrible for him and what he must have gone through.

She swallowed hard. That still didn't give him the right to do what he'd done to her… but somehow, she understood how someone could become that desperate. No wonder he started organizing the rogues.

"So, did your dad teach you to love art?"

She nodded. "He was a mechanic. Metal was his art. Then it became mine." She popped another piece of the cinnamon roll into her mouth. "What about you? What do you like to do?"

He shrugged. "I don't have much time for myself. Leading the Lycans and shifters takes a lot. Managing our investments takes a lot, too. But I like to ride and do outdoor things when I can."

"So you come up here often?"

He picked at a muffin. "Usually, I try to get out one weekend a month."

"For a little self-care. Nice."

"I don't know if it's self-care as much as it is to get away. To get back to nature. Back to my roots. Sometimes my uncle comes. He was there for me when my parents died."

"He seems… stern."

"He's a traditionalist. He believes in the laws of the pack and of the Lycan hierarchy. Everything he does is for the betterment of us as a race. Sometimes, he can come off as hard-nosed and unforgiving, but that's just his way. He's actually really kind and has been through a lot in his life. When my dad found my mom, she insisted that Osmodius come with her. They were very devoted to each other since their parents had died."

River ate the rest of her cinnamon roll and downed her soda before yawning.

"I can let you rest if you are still tired," he said.

"You know what I'd like to do is watch a movie, but I noticed there are no electronics up here."

"I like the solitude. I like having one place I can go to that the rest of the world can't get to." He looked at her for a moment. "But-"

"But?"

"I have an old TV and VHS player with some movies."

"I don't even know that I've ever seen a VHS player."

Apollo grabbed his heart. "Ouch. You make me feel so old."

"What movies do you have?" She snuggled into the covers.

He walked to the closet by the door and opened it. Inside, rows and rows of VHS tapes stood perfectly lined up.

"What did you do, buy out a Blockbuster before it went out of business?"

"Oh, so you know what a Blockbuster store is, but not a VHS?"

"I didn't say I didn't know what a VHS player was; I said I'd never seen one before. So what all do you have in there?"

"Well, I have horror flicks. And action flicks. And finally, classic bad sci-fi movies."

"Wow. No romantic comedies?"

He snorted. "Would you want to watch one if I did?"

"No."

They both laughed

"What's your favorite movie?"

"I'm partial to *An American Werewolf in London.*"

"A werewolf movie? Isn't that kind of like a doctor who only watches medical dramas?"

"It makes me laugh to see what people think we are like. What about you? What do you like?"

"Honestly?"

"Of course."

"I like horror movies as well. Especially zombies and vampires. Or anything with Vincent Price. He, Christopher Lee, and Peter Cushing are classic."

His eyebrows raised. "I love Vincent Price movies. What's your favorite?"

"'Fall of the House of Usher,' and some of Edgar Alan Poe ones. Oh! And there is this one movie where Vincent Price has a daughter with poisoned blood because he doesn't want her to leave him."

"Twice Told Tales! That's a good one. I'm partial to The Raven."

She chuckled. "That's one's goofy. Like Comedy of Terrors."

"Love that one too."

"Do you have them?"

He smiled. "Of course."

River nodded. "Okay, let's watch them."

He cocked an eyebrow at her.

She shrugged. "You have somewhere else you'd rather be?"

He smiled. "Absolutely not."

CHAPTER EIGHT

RIVER

After two gruesome Vincent Price movies, a knock sounded on the door, and Apollo hopped up to get it. He opened the door a hair, and a hand with two shopping bags slid in through the crack.

"Thank you, Bennett."

"Of course."

Apollo closed the door and turned back to her, holding up the bags. "Sorry, they only have a thrift store in town."

She shrugged. "Clothes are clothes. Used are better, in my opinion, because they are softer, and you can tell what they will fit like since they've been washed several times."

A strange expression planted on his face.

"What?"

He shook his head. "You are different from any female I've ever met."

"Thank you."

He snorted and sat on the bed with the bags. She dumped them out and looked at everything. Bennett had done a pretty good job of guessing her sizing, except for the underwear. A new pack of women's underwear with a sticker from the general store indicated that it was size XL. She pulled out a pair and held them up.

"I'm curvy, but I'm not big sexy curvy."

Apollo burst out laughing.

She threw the underwear at him. "If you think they are so funny, you wear them."

"Okay." Apollo stripped off his sweats before stepping into the underwear.

Okay, so he goes commando. Good to know.

River burst out laughing. The underwear barely hugged the hips of his large frame.

"You like them?" Apollo cat-walked back and forth, and River laughed even harder.

She couldn't remember the last time she'd laughed so hard. She laughed and then snorted, and Apollo stopped.

"You snort?"

She snorted again.

"Oh my gosh. You snort when you laugh. That's hilarious."

She couldn't help but laugh harder, which made her snort more. She couldn't stop.

Apollo looked down. "Okay. I don't look that funny in these."

She nodded, and tears streamed out of her eyes as she laughed.

“You’d better stop, or I might get a complex. I've never had a woman laugh at my physique before."

"Did they ever see you in lacy purple granny panties?"

He shook his head solemnly. "No, Kitten, this fantastic sight I saved just for you."

She dried her eyes and giggled a few more times. "Well, it's a sight I will never forget, but also one I never need to see again."

A wicked twinkle settled in his eyes. "Does that mean you want me to take them off?"

"Of course."

"Okay. If you want me naked..." He reached for the waistband.

"That's not... I mean... Yes, take them off, but put your sweats back on."

He tsked. "You are no fun at all."

"I'm tons of fun."

"Okay, let's do something fun then."

"A board game?"

He nodded.

"I'll play a board game, but only if I get to pick the next movie."

Apollo smiled his amazing crooked grin. "Deal."

APOLLO

After River beat Apollo three consecutive times in three separate games, he decided it was time to try something else.

"Want to go outside for a run?"

Apollo watched River for a minute, thinking she might say no. But finally, she stood and stretched.

"A run would be nice. Who knows how long it'll be until I can run again."

"What do you mean?" Apollo asked.

"I mean, I don't know anything about the estate. I don't know if I can run there. I don't know if it's safe. I don't know if I have to go somewhere else. Who knows if you'll have ten million bodyguards watching me so I can never go."

They walked outside and waited until they'd gotten into the trees before changing out of their clothes. Despite all that had happened between them, River was still modest and insisted he go behind a tree while she changed. It made him smile.

He couldn't believe her mom put her through so much, and then after that, not even knowing that you're an Omega, only to find out because somebody bit you. He couldn't imagine what that would be like.

"I'm done," River called.

"Almost finished."

He heard a shuffling noise, and then he shifted. When he peeked around the tree, she stood in her beautiful silvery glory. He'd never seen a more beautiful wolf in his entire life. To Apollo, she was everything. She walked up to him tentatively, stopped, and then nipped at his front leg before darting off with a chuff.

Oh, so that's how the run's gonna go.

His wolf howled in delight.

The chase was on.

RIVER MAY NOT HAVE SPENT MUCH TIME RUNNING IN WOLF FORM, but she'd taken to it like she'd been doing it since she was a child. Every time Apollo went to pounce on her, she would dart away or fake a turn. They spent over an hour with him trying to catch her. In frustration, he shifted back to human and tackled her.

She wiggled to get out of his grip, but couldn't. Eventually, she gave up and refused to look at him.

"Oh, you think I cheated, huh?" he teased.

She huffed.

"It's not my fault you're too fast for me."

She still refused to look at him.

"Is it because I'm naked again? Is that why you won't look at me?"

She yawned.

"Well, thank you very much. It's good to know that my being naked doesn't entice you at all."

She looked at him, and he grinned. "Tag. You're it."

He jumped up and shifted midair before tearing off into the trees. He looked over his shoulder to see her flip to her feet and beeline straight for him.

Apollo and his wolf were sure they'd never done anything as fun in their entire lives.

RIVER

River chased Apollo until her legs gave out, and she fell to the mossy ground, exhausted but thrilled. She'd never been an exerciser and definitely not a runner, but somehow, in wolf form, there was nothing better than running.

As the sun began to set under the mountains, she lay on her side and took in the scents and feel of the woods. It felt all too natural, too right. She could see herself living like that permanently-no cell phones, no computers, just… peace. Peace, joy, and Apollo.

Apollo trotted up behind her and dropped to the ground, setting his head on hers. The feel of his warm body against hers made River smile. It was so comfortable with him. So easy. Nothing like with Ares, who was all fire and passion. Apollo was the part of her she'd never experienced before. A part she'd never even known she missed. The comfortable, protected, loved part. The part that made life easier. When she'd thought of finding a mate growing up, this was what she'd expected. Someone who just felt like he'd always been there. A confidant. A protector. And someone she knew she could rely on for anything.

They lay together, staring up at the sky. She sucked in a breath and chuffed.

Apollo shifted. “Wow. The Northern Lights. You can see them here sometimes. Not in the city too often, but here, they are visible when the weather is right. It's been years since I've seen them this far south, though.”

She chuffed.

They stared at the sky, and Apollo rubbed her side for nearly an hour. The beautiful rainbow of greens and blues that floated across the sky made her wish she painted.

Apollo kissed her head. "Are you hungry?"

River whined.

"I'm gonna run to the cabin and tell them to grab dinner. I think something meaty would be best. Steaks, maybe."

River licked her lips.

He ruffled her ear and kissed her nose. "I'll be back in twenty. Don't run off without me."

She rolled back over and watched the lights flutter across the sky like colored mist. She wished she could capture the sight and hold onto it forever.

Her eyelids grew heavy, and she closed her eyes, allowing the evening breeze to wash over her. She'd not known peace like that in so many years that she'd forgotten it was an option.

RIVER AWOKE TO THE SNAPPING OF A TWIG. HER EYES FLEW OPEN, and it took her a moment to realize where she was. Had she fallen asleep? How long had she been there?

Another twig snapped, and she lifted her head.

Apollo?

She scanned for him, but he was nowhere in sight. She sniffed the air, but couldn't tell what she smelled. It didn't smell like a wolf, but it didn't smell human, either. It smelled… of nothing.

She jumped to her feet and listened. She had no idea where they were in relation to the cabins, but she didn't want to stay put. Her wolf paced, telling her they should run. But which direction?

Whispering caught her attention. She spotted them in the dusk. What the hell were they doing on Apollo and Ares' land? She stepped back, trying to hide behind a thick bush. Then she caught the glint of a gun.

Hunters.

River tried backing up further but hit a root and stumbled.

"Did you hear that?" one of the hunters asked.

River froze.

"There she is," said the other.

"Where?"

"There. By the tree."

She? They were looking for her?

River looked closer as the men emerged from the shadows into the low light. She recognized one of them. The man from the street. The one who'd stared at her. A bandage covered his nose, and he had two black eyes, but he wore the same clothes.

She wondered if Apollo had broken his nose. Maybe he wasn't as innocent as she thought.

She sniffed the air again, and again, the strange, muted scent of nothingness struck her. Similar to how she'd not smelled Titan when he'd scratched her. And just like that time, her wolf told her there was a problem.

Though her wolf begged her to run, River didn't move a muscle.

"Shoot her already so we can get out of here," said the one with the broken nose.

The other man raised his gun and aimed at River.

Oh, hell no!

She was not going out like that. Shot by human assholes. River growled and then leapt toward them.

A shot rang out, and something whooshed over her head and struck the tree behind her. She hurled herself onto the man with the gun in a heartbeat. She grabbed his arm, ripping and tearing into it, crushing the bones in her teeth. The man screamed, and with a whip of her head, she tore the limb from his body and flung it away.

"Holy shit!" The man with the broken nose yelled.

The first man rolled on the ground, wailing and grabbing at his torn flesh.

The second man backed up a step, and then his form rippled, but nothing happened. He tried again and again, but nothing happened.

"Damn Titan!"

A chill raced down River's spine. Titan. He'd sent the men to find her. But they weren't men. They were shifters.

River lunged at him, teeth bared, and he pulled a pistol from his hoodie.

"Stay back."

River growled, and her hackles raised. She stalked forward as he continued to back up.

Kill. Kill. Kill.

"I mean it. I don't care what Titan says. I will shoot you if you come any closer."

Titan again. The Lycan ruining her life.

Not this time.

River howled and prepared to leap when a dark blur came out of the trees and knocked the shifter to the ground. The man fell flat on his belly, and the gun slid out of his hand.

The colossal wolf ripped into the man's shoulder with a crunch. The man screamed and scrambled forward, reaching for the gun. River lunged, but he grabbed the gun and fired once.

She didn't hear the shot, but she felt the explosion that ripped through her shoulder.

Her wolf cried out and backed up. She stumbled and struggled on three paws.

Apollo roared and shifted into his human form before grabbing the man and slamming him against the nearest tree. The man crumpled to the ground, and Apollo picked him up and slammed him into the tree again before transforming again and ripping the man's head off.

River whined as pain continued to shoot through her like wildfire.

Dammit. She shouldn't have been so stupid. She should have

run. Ares would lose it when he found out. Ares would blame Apollo. She remembered Ares' promise to kill Apollo if anything happened to her.

Apollo stalked over to the first man and shifted back to human. "Who told you that you could hunt on my land?"

The man's mouth opened and closed, but no noise came out.

"Answer me!" he demanded, shaking the man.

"Titan told us to come."

"To kill her?"

"No. To take her to him."

Apollo roared. "Titan." He slashed the man from groin to chest, and the man's gut spilled onto the ground.

Apollo threw the man into a tree, breaking his neck, before turning to River. Blood slicked his skin, tinging every inch of him in red. The sight both terrified and excited her. She whimpered, and he rushed to her side, looking her over and touching her gently.

"I'm so sorry, Kitten. I didn't think-" He cut off as emotion filled his eyes. "I should never have left you."

He bowed his head and pressed a kiss to her muzzle. "I'm so sorry."

She breathed in and winced as pain shot through her shoulder.

Without a word, he gathered her in his arms and cradled her to his solid chest before taking off.

CHAPTER NINE

APOLLO

Apollo raced for the cabins. He was still close to a hundred yards away when he started screaming for Bennett.

Bennett, Silas, Regan, Thomas, and Lachlan came running, guns already out.

"Bennett! Get the med kit."

Silas jumped the stairs and raced to them. "What happened?"

"It's Titan."

Regan and Thomas shifted and tore off in different directions.

Apollo approached the cabin, and Lachlan ran up to them.

"No. No. No. Oh shit. Ares is going to kill me," he said.

"Get in line," Apollo growled.

He kicked open the cabin door and ran to the couch. Gently as he could, he laid River on the fabric before running to get her a blanket. He returned, and his mind couldn't focus. The scent of her blood sent his wolf into a frenzy. Killing the men hadn't been enough. He should have done more. Worse.

"What happened?"

They'd shot her. His River. Apollo's wolf wanted to hunt down Titan and rip him limb from limb.

"Highness," Bennett entered with a kit.

Apollo looked up at him.

"May I look at her?" Bennett asked.

Apollo continued to stare for a minute, and then he backed away.

Bennett approached her carefully and knelt by the couch. He lifted the blanket, and Apollo growled.

Bennett stopped and looked at Apollo. "This might be easier if you left."

"No," he bellowed.

Bennett didn't flinch.

"Maybe put some pants on then?" he offered.

River shook with pain. Apollo reached for her and kissed her paw. "I'm not leaving her again. Not for a minute."

Bennett sighed and looked to River. "I'm sorry, Highness, but I must look at your wound. Is that all right?"

Apollo growled, but River nodded.

Bennett picked up the blanket, now soaked in blood, and spread her fur to inspect her shoulder.

She cried out.

Apollo grabbed Bennett's arm, his nails lengthening.

Bennett looked down at Apollo's grip and then into his eyes. "I need to see if the bullet is still in there." His voice and eyes remained calm.

Apollo let go. His brain screamed that these things needed to be done, but his wolf wanted no part of it. He waited so close to the surface that Apollo almost couldn't control the shift ripples wracking his body.

"It's still in there," said Bennett.

Apollo let out a string of curses so loud that the windows shook.

"I'm sorry, Kitten."

Bennett and Apollo changed places, and Apollo stroked her mane. Apollo closed his eyes and bowed his head next to River's. How could he have let this happen? He had just found her and already couldn't take care of her. Maybe he'd be better off letting Ares have her. Ares never would have let something like this happen. Hadn't let something like this happen. Even when outnumbered at the theater.

River nudged him with her nose and then licked his forehead.

He looked up at her bright green eyes.

"I have the tools," said Bennett. "I can get it out, but it won't feel good. I think it's best if you… leave."

Apollo went to protest, but Bennett stopped him. "Apollo, do you want me to do it right, or do you want me to do it when my wolf is scared you are going to bite his head off at her slightest discomfort?"

Bennett was right, but his wolf didn't want to comply.

"I have an idea that can keep us busy while he works," said Silas. "Something to take the edge off for you and your wolf."

Apollo looked at River again. He couldn't leave her.

Mine. My mate. No males. Mine.

I can't stand to hear her in pain. I'll kill Bennett if we don't go.

No, go! Stay. Protect.

Apollo swallowed hard. *I am protecting her and us. If we hurt him, she will never forgive herself or us, and neither will we. We must go to protect her.*

She nudged him with her nose, and he dug his fingers into her silky mane. He kissed her face before standing and backing away.

His wolf bellowed, but he forced himself to move away.

"I'll stay with her," Lachlan offered.

Stupid pup. Didn't he know that was the absolute wrong thing to say?

Silas laid his hand on Apollo's shoulder and pulled Apollo out the door.

River's gaze never left his until he hit the exit, and the screen door swung closed.

He stood for a moment, fighting every instinct to rush back to her side.

She whimpered, and he turned.

Silas grabbed him around the chest. "Don't. It will only hurt both of you even more."

Apollo's wolf rushed to the surface and banged against his restraints, almost snapping them.

"I have to-"

Silas yanked Apollo away from the door, and Apollo turned on him and grabbed him by the throat. He bared his fangs and roared.

Silas stared at him but didn't react.

River. River. My River.

A moment passed, and then another, and Apollo dropped Silas to his feet. He removed his hand from Silas' throat and growled.

“What's your plan?"

RIVER

River breathed a sigh of relief when Apollo exited the cabin. Physical pain was one thing, but dealing with his emotional pain, anger, and guilt on top of that was something she couldn't handle. Not mixed with her own.

"Highness," said Bennett. "It'll be easier to get the bullets out if you shift back to your human form."

She nodded and tried to shift, but her wolf refused to give up control. She tried again and again, but her wolf refused. River tried reasoning with her, but that didn't work. So, finally, River did the only thing left- the thing she only did if absolutely necessary. She hated it, but this was for both of them.

River commanded her wolf to back down. For a moment, she didn't think her wolf would, but then she relinquished control.

River shifted to human. It took longer than it should have, leaving her panting in agony. A fine sheen of sweat developed on her skin, and nausea rolled through her.

"Hello, Highness," said Bennett.

"Call me River."

"I wouldn't dare, Highness. I am medically trained and can take the bullets out, but it will hurt."

She nodded. "Okay."

"Would you like a drink?"

She snorted. "I'd have to drink a whole bottle to give you even twenty minutes."

"Lachlan, grab the whiskey while I transfer her to the table."

Lachlan headed somewhere out of sight as Bennett prepared to touch her.

"May I lift you, Highness?"

"You know I've been asked if I can be touched, talked to, and called by something other than my name more in the last week than in my twenty-four years of life."

"That's because it's different now. You are the Alpha's mate. The King of Lycans. To do any of those things without his say-so is grounds for immediate execution."

"Seriously?"

Bennett nodded.

"Well, I don't want that to happen, so yes, you have my permission to do whatever you need to keep yourself and me alive."

He slipped his arms underneath her, carefully ensuring the blanket covered every inch he touched.

"This isn't going to be comfortable, I'm afraid."

He stood, and pain ripped through her. She grabbed his shirt with her good hand and hissed.

“It’s going to be okay, Princess.”

Bennett carried her to the kitchen table, laying her on her back.

River continued to focus on breathing for several seconds before finally releasing Bennet’s shirt.

“I know it’s not comfortable,” said Bennett. “But I need a hard surface to work effectively.”

“I’ve slept on worse,” she said. That wasn't necessarily the truth. After what Titan had done to her, her mom had sewn her up on the kitchen counter. That hadn’t been comfortable either. It had taken weeks for her to fully heal because of the suppressors. She’d found out at that time that they didn’t just suppress her wolf, they suppressed all of her shifter abilities- including quick healing.

A memory hit her. That's why the shifter cursed Titan when he'd been trying to shift. He couldn't because of suppressors.

Lachlan approached with a bottle and a shot glass. He poured the amber liquid into the glass and shakily held it out to her. It slopped out the side of the glass, and she laid her hand on his.

"Lachlan. You take that shot."

"But, Highness-"

"River."

"It's for you."

"And I command you to drink it."

He didn't argue; he gulped it down and poured another.

"That one too."

He did as he was told.

"I need you calm to keep me calm."

Lachlan nodded.

"All right. Hand me the bottle."

He hesitated for only a second before handing it to her. She took a deep breath, then slammed the bottle to her lips, and gulped four times in quick order before taking a breath that made the fire in her lungs rival her shoulder.

Bennett entered with a bag and opened it on the counter. He pulled out several tools and then walked back to the table. He looked at the bottle and nodded.

River returned his nod, her head already fuzzing over. She grabbed Lachlan's hand, and Bennett looked at it before uncovering her shoulder.

"Ready?"

No. River nodded.

The pain exploded as if she'd been shot all over again. She gripped Lachlan's hand so tightly he grimaced.

"Wow. You're strong."

She snorted.

Another pain shot through her, and she squeezed his hand again.

"Almost got it," said Bennett. "It's not as bad as I thought."

"You should feel it." River gritted her teeth. Her wolf yelped and whined in pain.

Come on, you big baby. You didn't even want to relinquish control. If I'd let you stay in charge, you'd have bitten Bennett's throat.

Minutes passed, and she began to sweat again, and her body shook.

"We're almost done," said Lachlan. "It'll just be another-"

"Got it."

A slight metal clink hit the table, and River's body relaxed. She gulped down air like she'd been underwater.

Bennett poured the alcohol into her wound, and River roared. He pressed a cotton pad to her shoulder and taped it down. Then he gathered the instruments, walked into the kitchen, and cleaned them in a sink.

She reached for the whiskey bottle, and Lachlan helped her bring it shakily to her mouth. Again, she gulped down several fiery mouthfuls.

Bennett returned. "How ya doing, Highness?"

"Not dead yet."

He smiled. "Let's keep it that way for all of our sakes."

Her eyes closed and then opened again. She'd not had that much to drink that fast since she'd turned nineteen.

She blinked up at the men peering down at her, vaguely recognizing one of them as her vision began to swim. “Lachlan?"

"Yes, Highness."

Her mind wandered, and she fought to remember where she was. "Where's Ares?"

"Uh…" He looked at her and then at the other guy.

She looked at the man. "Who are you again?"

"Bennett, Highness. I am Prince Apollo's friend."

She repeated the name. "Apollo. Apollo. Ares. Ares and Apollo are twins."

"Yes, Highness," said Lachlan.

"I… I have to choose."

"Yes, Highness. But not now."

"I… I think I'm going to choose Ares."

Again, the men exchanged a look she couldn't decipher. "Why do you keep doing that?"

"What, Highness?" asked Bennett.

"You keep staring at each other like you know something I don't."

River tried to focus but couldn't remember what they'd been talking about.

"I don't like being drunk," she said right before passing out.

APOLLO

Apollo approached the cabin with Silas in tow. He stopped outside the door and listened, but no sound emanated. He opened the door and looked inside to find Lachlan and Bennett at the table, talking quietly. They turned when they heard the door.

He sniffed and smelled River's blood mixed with antiseptic and alcohol.

"Did you get it out?"

Bennett nodded. "She's resting in the bedroom."

"I want to see her." He headed for the room, but Lachlan stood and blocked the way.

Apollo growled.

"I beg your pardon, Highness, but… maybe you might consider showering first?"

"He's right," said Silas. "If you go in covered in… everything we are covered in, you might scare her to death."

Apollo looked down at the blood, soot, and dirt that stained his skin. He looked at the bedroom door. He smelled her in there and heard her steady heartbeat. She slept deeply.

Without a word, he headed to the bathroom and turned on the shower.

IT TOOK ALMOST TEN MINUTES FOR THE WATER TO WARM, BUT Apollo let it rain on him anyway, cooling his waning rage.

Silas' idea had been a good one. They hadn't located the hunters' scents, so finding their way to where they'd been staying had taken close to an hour. Eventually, the smell of cooking food led him to the place he'd been looking for.

Inside, he'd found half a dozen other rogues whom he'd ripped to pieces after interrogating them. None of them seemed to know where Titan was. Only the one whom Apollo had broken the nose of earlier and later killed had known anything.

After killing the last rogue and burning the cabin to the ground , he felt mildly better. Going back to the original attackers, ripping their bodies into small pieces, and tossing them over the cliff had made him feel considerably better. He only wished he could have done it twice.

He washed himself, being careful to get all the gore from under his nails and out of his scalp. Then he stepped from the shower and brushed his teeth before running his fingers through his hair and trying to find something to wear. Bennett and Silas had gone, most likely to patrol, but Lachlan remained behind.

"You may go." He spotted some folded clothes on the kitchen counter, grabbed them, and put them on.

"If it's all right, Highness, I'd like to stay."

Apollo wanted to argue, but all the fight had left him for the evening.

Regan and Thomas entered.

"Anything?"

They shook their heads. "We'll ask around town tomorrow."

Apollo nodded. "Stay out there and keep watch. If you have any problems, find Bennett."

Apollo walked to the bedroom and opened the door quietly. He peered into the darkness and could make out River's small form curled under the covers. He sniffed the air and caught the scent of her already healing wound.

He backed out but stopped when she called his name.

"Apollo?"

"I didn't mean to wake you."

"Would you mind getting me some water?"

"Of course not."

He rushed into the kitchen and grabbed a bottle from the fridge.

He walked to the bed and sat on it before opening the bottle and holding it to her lips. She took several long drinks, then sucked in a deep breath.

"How are you feeling?"

"I've been better. But I've also been worse."

He set the bottle on the nightstand and lifted her hand to his lips, kissing it. "Can you ever forgive me?"

She patted his cheek. "I don't blame you."

"I would understand if you told me to take you back to Ares immediately."

She lifted his chin to look at her. "Will you stay while I sleep?"

His wolf howled at her request.

How could she want that when he'd let her get hurt and almost killed?

Apollo curled beside her, careful not to touch her.

"Where did you go with Silas?" she asked mid-yawn.

He swallowed hard. She didn't need to know the full details.

"We disposed of the bodies and covered our tracks."

"You smell more like smoke than usual," she said. "Did you burn them?"

He brushed her hair with his fingers and kissed her forehead. "Sleep. We can talk in the morning."

She inched backward until her body made contact with his, and then she lifted his arm and wrapped it around her, linking her fingers with his.

"I like how you smell," she murmured.

CHAPTER TEN

RIVER

River awoke stiff and sore. The sunlight filtered through the curtains, and she wondered how long she'd been asleep. She rolled over, and her shoulder winced.

The door opened, and Apollo peeked his head in. He walked to her and pushed her tangled hair from her face. "How are you?"

"Tired. Sore. How about you?"

His face took on a perplexed expression. "I'm doing fine."

He looked at her shoulder, and his expression turned to sadness and anger.

"It's not your fault."

He shook his head but wouldn't meet her eye.

She lifted his chin so he looked at her. "It's not your fault."

He searched her face for a moment and then smiled at her. "Hungry?"

She narrowed her eyes. "Wait… Have you been checking on me every five minutes to see if I was awake?"

"No."

"Then how did you know I just woke up?"

A smile played across his lips, and he rubbed the back of his neck. "Uh… because the snoring stopped?"

"Snoring?" she said, horrified. "I do not snore."

"Of course not. You're right. I've just been coming in every five minutes."

She threw her hand over her face. How embarrassing could things get? Shot by a rogue. Drunk in front of Bennett and Lachlan. She said things she couldn't remember but was sure were embarrassing because she remembered them looking at each other several times. And now snoring in front of… well, everyone with wolf hearing.

"It's not a big deal. If it makes you feel better, you didn't drool."

She looked at him. "No. It doesn't."

He snorted. "I have no idea why snoring is such a big deal for females. Wait till I'm exhausted. I've been told my snoring can be heard on the other side of the estate."

She chuckled.

"Maybe I shouldn't have told you that. I am trying to win you over, after all."

"Don't worry. I'm not a light sleeper."

His eyes glittered, and he shoved his hands in his pockets. "So, food? I can send out for something. Whatever you want. Or we can go to the diner. Find a hamburger place. You name it."

Her stomach growled. "Bakery stuff sounds great. And also, maybe a hamburger. And the largest cola out there? Or two?"

He inclined his head. "Your wish is my command, Kitten." He winked at her and backed out of the room.

She sat up stiffly and caught a glimpse of herself in the mirror across from the bed. Oh man, she needed a brush, or ten, to tame her crazy hair. She tried to run her fingers through it, but couldn't even get them through an inch.

She was so screwed.

River slid off the bed and looked through the bags on the floor, cradling her injured arm against her. She picked a pair of terry-cloth shorts and a heavy-metal band T-shirt. Apollo knocked and then re-entered. River stood with the clothes.

"Let me help you with those." He ripped the tags off for her and then helped slip the T-shirt over her head.

She winced, lifting her arm, but refused to let Apollo see her pain as he helped slide it through the armhole. He blamed himself enough.

"Sorry, Kitten."

"You need to stop apologizing."

"I can't. Your pain is my fault."

"No. My pain is the fault of the rogues who thought they could grab me for Titan."

Apollo growled, and his eyes grew black.

She tried to remember what happened the night before. She'd been in the woods, and two rogues had shown up. What had they said?

Her wolf growled.

"How did he know I was out here?" she mused.

"He had rogues watching the town. He obviously knew about our family land. He was born here as well, I believe. They saw you and waited until you were alone."

"They couldn't shift. I think Titan had them on blockers like my mom used to make me take."

He nodded. "Titan is getting desperate and smarter. Using the blockers masked their scents from me as well."

"When I first heard them, and then tried to smell them, they smelled like… nothing."

"That's what blockers do. In crowds or packs, it isn't noticeable because the other shifters mask the nothingness. But it's more noticeable one-on-one or in a group of two or three. Though blockers usually don't mask shifters from Lycans. So I should have been able to smell them."

She nodded and then remembered something. "The one that saw me in town looked like he had a broken nose; that was you, wasn't it?"

"If I'd known then that he was more than a human, I'd have ended him instead," Apollo growled. "I'm-"

She pressed her finger to his lips. "Stop. They are gone, and I'm healing, so please stop apologizing. As far as Titan knows, they are still waiting, right? So it's fine."

His eyes began to clear. "How can you be so forgiving?"

"I place blame where blame is due. You didn't hurt me any more than Ares did when we were attacked in New York. Honestly, I thought Titan would still be in New York. If I'd thought he was in Canada, I'd have been much more cautious."

"So would I."

She touched his chest. "I know you would have. Neither of us could have guessed he'd find us out here."

He touched her cheek. "Maybe we should go back to the estate. You're safer there."

"No. I don't want him to ruin our time together. We can just stay in the cabin until it's time to leave. Order in. Watch movies. Play games."

"If that's what you wish."

"It is."

He handed her the shorts, and she pulled them on while he turned away.

"Lachlan went for food. He should be back shortly. What would you like to do in the meantime?"

She caught a glimpse of herself in the mirror again. "Uh... you don't happen to have a hairbrush?"

He walked out of the room and returned a moment later with a brush.

She took her time sectioning off her hair and trying to brush it, but without using both hands, she couldn't make much headway.

"May I?"

"Thank you." She handed him the brush, and he sat behind her, wrapping his long legs on either side of hers.

He started at the bottom and worked his way up. Cocooned in his powerful thighs, her thoughts heated.

He brushed the hair from her neck, sending a shiver down her skin. His scent swirled around her, and she remembered the feel of his body next to hers the night before. Her cheeks flushed, and his warm breath tickled her neck.

"You are so beautiful, Kitten." His lips brushed her skin, and she stifled a moan.

Then, as quick as he kissed her, he sat back and continued to brush her hair.

Tease.

THIRTY MINUTES LATER, APOLLO FINISHED HER HAIR AND PULLED IT into a scrunchie. She'd never been a scrunchie type of girl, but she didn't want to deal with a mass of tangles again by bedtime.

A knock on the door sounded, and Apollo opened it. Lachlan handed him the food, but his gaze landed on River.

"What's wrong?" Apollo asked.

Lachlan looked between them and shook his head. "Nothing, Highness." His eyes drifted to River again; she thought he wanted to talk to her.

"Well, if it's nothing, then goodbye." Apollo closed the door in Lachlan's face.

He returned to the bed and set the bag of muffins down before handing her a gigantic soda.

She took a gulp. "Why don't you like Lachlan?"

He stopped opening the food bags. "Because he's not loyal to me. He's loyal to Ares."

"He can't be loyal to both of you?"

Apollo's gaze met hers. "No. Loyalty is always slightly stronger to one Alpha or the other."

She knew he wasn't just talking about Lachlan. She dropped her gaze, and her thoughts turned to Ares. She wondered what he was going through. What was he doing right then? Was he thinking of her? Had he worked out his pent-up energy with another female?

Her wolf snarled at the thought.

No. He had meetings and things to attend to. He was the Prince, after all. And he's just had meetings in New York. Of course, he didn't have time to sit around pining for her. Besides, from what she could tell, there weren't any other females in the estate besides herself.

Her wolf whined.

River sighed.

"I'm sorry. I didn't mean to remind you of the real reason you are here. I just want you to understand."

She looked up at him. "If you apologize to me again, I'm going to bite you."

A wry smile played on his lips. "Promise?"

She hadn't meant it to come out like that; even so, the idea didn't repulse her. She sipped her soda. She had never understood people who wanted to be with more than one person. She always knew as a shifter that she would find a mate, and that would be it. They would be together forever. However, that wasn't how things were playing out for her. It shouldn't have surprised her. Nothing in her life had ever been simple.

For the first time, she wondered if she could choose between them and what would happen if she couldn't.

CHAPTER ELEVEN

RIVER

They were finishing an action movie just after noon when a vehicle approached the cabin at high speed. Apollo jumped off the bed and rushed to the door.

"Stay here."

He'd barely pulled it open when a set of heavy footsteps stormed into the cabin, and a familiar voice rang out.

"River!" Ares called.

Apollo looked at her, and his body relaxed before he threw a tight smile and closed the bedroom door. Loud, yet muffled voices sailed through the wall.

"Where is she?" Ares demanded. "River? Where are you?"

"You aren't supposed to be here," Apollo said.

"And what? I should just leave my mate with you to die?"

"My mate is doing just fine. She is resting, and your shouting won't make her any better."

"Where is she?" Ares growled.

"You need to leave."

Feet scuffled, and then a roar shook the walls.

River scooted to the edge of the bed and hurried to the door. She opened it to find Ares and Apollo fighting.

Again?

"Ares," she called. "Ares, stop!"

Immediately, Ares turned to her, shoved Apollo to the floor, and ran to where she stood. He stopped short of pulling her into a hug and instead leaned in and sniffed her.

A whine escaped his lips. "Beloved," he whispered.

He lowered his head to her neck and sniffed her injured shoulder.

"Show me."

She pulled the T-shirt collar down, revealing the large bandage. He tugged at the medical tape and looked at the wound.

"It isn't healed yet. Why isn't it healed?" Worry tinged his voice, bordering on panic.

"It won't be healed for a day or so."

"But-"

"I'm a shifter, not Lycan. I heal slower."

He nodded and dropped to his knees. River's gaze connected with Apollo's. He barely held it together.

Ares wrapped his arms around her waist and rested his head on her stomach.

She'd just touched his hair when he jumped to his feet again.

"You did this. This is your fault." He took a step toward Apollo, but River grabbed his hand.

"No. It's my fault."

Both men looked at her.

"I… I wanted to sleep out there. And when the rogues arrived, I… got confused. I didn't realize what they were."

"But-"

"It's my fault," she insisted.

Ares turned to her and cupped her face. "Why are you covering for him?"

"I'm not," she said firmly. "If you want to blame someone else, blame Titan. He's the one who sent them."

Ares growled, and his eyes turned black. "Titan's here?"

"No," said Apollo. "I don't think they'd told him they'd found her yet."

"They?"

"A house full of rogues waited to see if we'd show."

Ares searched her face, emotions playing all over his features.

She wanted to comfort him. Let him know she was all right, but she couldn't. Not in front of Apollo. It felt… wrong.

"We're going home," Ares announced.

"No." Apollo stepped forward. "The council said-"

"The council changed their minds. Seeing as you cannot protect *my mate*, they've agreed you should return to the estate."

Apollo rushed to Ares so fast that River didn't see him move. He shoved Ares against the wall.

"Stop calling her that. She's not just your mate. She's mine, too. And I will not let you take her. I don't care what the council says. I am the king. The Alpha of Alphas and my word is final."

Ares pushed Apollo off. "You aren't the king yet. Not until you take a mate."

"Well, that's only a matter of time, isn't it? I've already chosen, and now it's up to her to choose."

The men stood nose to nose.

"River." Ares held his hand out to her without looking.

Her wolf whined, and she looked from Ares to Apollo and back.

"River." Apollo held out his hand.

Seriously? Were they doing this? After all she'd been through?

Anger flared. She would not be a pawn in their dick-measuring contest.

Her wolf growled. *No. Choose.*

Exactly.

"I think I'll take a nap." Before either could say anything, she walked into the bedroom, slammed the door, and locked it.

APOLLO

When River opened the bedroom door two hours later, Apollo looked up from where he sat on the couch and waited for her to come to him.

Ares showing up threw a wrench in his plans in a big way, but the fact that she hadn't immediately gone with him was a win in Apollo's book, and he would take it. Though she'd made it clear she wasn't happy with either of them for trying to make her choose.

Her soft footsteps padded down the hallway toward him. When she entered the front room, he stood.

"Did you sleep?"

She nodded and wrapped her arm around her middle.

"Can I get you anything?"

She shook her head. He grabbed a throw from the back of the couch and walked to her, wrapping it around her shoulders.

"Thank you," she said dryly.

His hands lingered on her arms. "It's I who needs to thank you."

"For what?"

"Lying to Ares. We both know it's my fault."

Her brow furrowed. "I told the truth."

"But if I hadn't left-"

"Then maybe you would have been shot first. I would be dead if it weren't for you coming when you did."

He searched her face, but it remained a mask.

She looked around. "Where are Ares and the others?"

"In different cabins. They all refused to leave."

She pushed her hair behind her ear. "Do you know how he found out?"

"I have an idea," he growled.

She nodded. "Lachlan."

"He went into town to get the food, and Ares showed up an hour later."

She blew out a harsh breath. Damn, she wished Lachlan hadn't done that. It would make it that much harder for Apollo to like him.

"I'm sorry. I shouldn't have asked him to come."

"Trust me, any of Ares' guards would have done the same as would mine."

The tension released from her posture a fraction.

"River, I want to apologize for earlier. It was wrong of me to try to make you choose between Ares and myself. It was-"

"Egotistical?"

"Yes."

"Childish?"

"Definitely."

"Selfish?"

"Absolutely." He nodded.

Her shoulders sagged, and she gave him a sad smile. "Thank you."

He took her hand and kissed her knuckles.

"So… do we have to go back?"

Her use of the words 'have to' made his wolf smile. "That's up to you."

"Won't the council get mad?"

"They can get mad all they want, but ultimately, it's your decision, and they won't go against what you want."

She chewed the inside of her cheek.

"Would you like to go back?"

She sucked in a large breath. "I like it here. I like the quiet. It reminds me of home."

"Of Soho?"

"No. The home where my dad raised me."

He couldn't help but smile.

She stepped forward and laid her head on his chest.

Apollo froze and then wrapped his arms around her small frame.

"I'm sorry Ares attacked you again," she said. "I don't want to come between you two."

"Trust me, we've had twenty-eight years' worth of things that came between us before you came along. And I'm sure there will be over twenty-eight years more."

He leaned in and kissed the top of her head. She looked up at him, her eyes alight. He ran his finger down her cheek, bent down, and gently pressed his lips to hers. Then he rubbed his nose against hers and pulled her into a hug again.

"I've wanted to do that since the first moment I smelled you," he said.

"Rub my nose against yours?"

His wolf chuffed.

"It's something my father used to do to my mother before he left on a trip."

Apollo lifted her chin. He bent in and kissed her again, but this time, he pressed his lips on hers more forcefully. He parted her lips with his tongue, and the taste of her swirled in his mouth, making his wolf howl. He tangled his fingers in her hair, and she pressed closer to him.

A white ribbon snaked around his wolf's ankle.

River gasped, and Apollo looked down at her, smiling. Their bond was strengthening.

"You feel it." He could barely get the words out.

She nodded, and he kissed her again. His. She was his, and he was hers. There was no denying it.

Mine. My Omega.

Apollo kissed her like it was the most essential thing in his life. He needed her to know and had to show her what she meant to him. To prove to her that he was the one for her.

A cough came from the doorway, and River stepped away.

Apollo growled and looked at the door. Lachlan held a bag.

"Uh… Prince Ares wanted me to bring the Princess something to eat. To help her highness heal quicker."

Of course, he did. More like he just wanted Lachlan to spy on them and report back.

"You brought us food earlier, remember?" said Apollo.

“Uh… yes. I did, but… uh…”

"Thank you," said River. "Why don't you put it on the table so Apollo and I can eat together?”

"I'm sure there's not enough for both of us."

She smiled. "Says who? Besides, if we are still hungry, we can send Silas or Bennett to get more while we watch your next favorite old horror movie."

ARES

ARES PACED THE CABIN, WAITING FOR LACHLAN TO RETURN. WHEN the door to the cabin opened, he raced to it.

"What happened?"

Lachlan looked up at him. "I gave her the food as you asked."

"What were they doing when you went in?"

Lachlan's eyes shifted away.

"What?" he demanded.

"Kissing."

Ares growled and slammed his fist into the cabin wall, splitting the wooden log. He was getting to her. His River. Once again, Apollo saw what Ares had and wanted to take it for himself.

Despair replaced his rage as he sank into the oversized chair he'd spent the last two hours in.

All he'd ever wanted was to find his true mate and raise a family with her. He didn't care about being Alpha. He didn't care about keeping the peace between the Lycans and shifters. He didn't even care about the estate. All he wanted was her. If she told him that she wanted to return to Soho the next day, he'd take her. If she said she wanted to elope, he'd do it. Whatever she wanted, he wanted to give it to her. It didn't matter. Nothing mattered. Nothing except for River.

CHAPTER TWELVE

RIVER

The next morning, River awoke to hushed voices speaking angrily in the front room. She got up feeling much better than in the past twenty-four hours.

She peeked under her bandage to find her wound mostly healed and now only bright red, so she removed the tape and dressings and threw them in the trash.

She grabbed a blanket and walked to the door. She pulled it open and heard Apollo arguing. She stepped into the hallway to find him talking to a man in a well-dressed suit, several inches shorter. The man's hands stayed clasped in front of him, and his face remained impassive. His gaze drifted to her as he noticed her and inclined his head.

Apollo looked at her.

"What's going on?"

He sighed and turned to the other man. "We'll be out in thirty minutes."

The man nodded and left.

"Who is that?"

Apollo ran his hands through his hair. "He's an emissary of the Council. They've ordered us to return to the estate."

"Why?"

"Because they want to hear what happened the other night from your lips. And because apparently…"

"Apparently, what?" Her heartbeat quickened.

"Your mom has arrived."

Her stomach plummeted. "Cherry's here?" She thought for a moment and then blew out a breath. "Bianca."

"Your sister, not sister?"

She nodded. "I'm sure Zeke found out from Ares and told her, and she called her dad. Prompting my mom to go haywire and travel to the estate." She groaned. "We should go. The longer she's there, the worse it will be for everyone."

"Of course."

River looked at Apollo. "I'm sorry."

He shrugged and shoved his hands in his pockets. "It is what it is. I just hope the time we shared was enough to give me a smidgeon of a chance."

THIRTY MINUTES LATER, RIVER AND APOLLO EXITED THE CABIN. Everyone was already waiting for them. Silas took her thrift store bags and put them in the trunk of Ares' car. Apollo walked to the car and opened the door for her.

"You don't want me to ride with you?" she asked.

"You're not fully healed. You'll be much more comfortable in the car."

He was so different than Ares. Where Ares was all demand and hot burning coals. Apollo was… sweet. Sensitive even. The kind of man who would be great with kids and not try to dominate her.

She looked up at Apollo and squeezed his hand. She wasn't sure what to say, so she simply said, 'Thank you,' and got in the car.

Apollo closed the door, and Ares sat beside her but didn't move to touch her. Her wolf whined and prodded River to connect with him. To say something. Do something. But River wasn't sure what to say. She was pretty sure Ares felt like she'd rejected him when she'd refused to leave with him the day before. It hadn't been her intention, but she hadn't said yes and went with him immediately like any other mate would have, because she wasn't ready to go back. Wasn't prepared to face what was coming. The Council. Having to decide…

After a minute, she scooted closer and laid her head on his shoulder. The car pulled off down the road, and his body shifted as he relaxed. He placed his hand on her lap. She clasped it in both hands, and he squeezed her fingers.

Her wolf sighed, contented, and laid down. River closed her eyes and sucked in Ares' familiar scent.

He kissed her head and began to purr. She moved her head to his lap and curled into a ball on the seat. He pulled the bun from the top of her head and massaged her scalp, making it tingle.

"I was so worried, Beloved."

She squeezed his leg and then kissed it. "I'm fine. And I'm right here. With you."

She couldn't help that nothing else seemed to matter when she was with him. And no one else, either.

He sighed. "As you will always be."

ARES HELPED RIVER OUT OF THE CAR WHEN THE FRONT DOOR OF the estate burst open.

River groaned.

Cherry raced outside, followed closely by Strider.

"You!" Cherry pointed at Ares. "I warned you what would happen if my daughter got hurt."

"Mom, it wasn't Ares' fault." But River's words had no effect. Her mom leapt at Ares from over ten feet away. She produced a knife midair, but before her mom could pounce on him, River stepped in the way and deflected her mom with a blow to the chest.

River groaned as the sudden movement ripped at her still-healing muscles.

Cherry fell backward and landed on the dirt. A moment later, the guards and Apollo pulled up on their bikes.

Cherry whipped to her feet. She took a step forward, and River did the same.

"I told you this isn't his fault. I wasn't even with him when it happened."

Apollo walked around the back of the car to stand on the other side of River. Cherry looked between them, and then Apollo stepped forward.

"I'm Apollo. You must be River's mother." He held out his hand, and Cherry slapped it away.

Apollo growled, but Cherry gave no notice. "So you're the asshole who let my daughter get shot."

"Yes," Apollo said. "I take the blame."

Cherry lashed out, but Apollo stepped out of the way. She lunged at him again, and again, he moved. Frustration grew in Cherry's eyes as she tried again to attack. This time, Silas stepped in front of her and grabbed her hand. Strider growled and shoved Silas.

"Stop," River yelled. "Everyone, just knock it the hell off already."

River took several steps forward before her leg cramped, and she stumbled. Ares caught her around the waist and lifted her into his arms.

"Can't you see she isn't fully healed yet?" Ares demanded. "You're hurting her with your fighting. Cherry, I know you are pissed. I'm pissed as well, but that isn't going to help River."

River looked at her mom and then to the others. "Please. Let's just go inside, and we can talk about this like civilized wolves."

Apollo looked at River in Ares' arms. "Put her down."

"You'd rather see her walk than have me carry her?" Ares retorted. When Apollo didn't answer, Ares swore. "You're such an asshole."

"I'll take her," offered Strider.

Both Apollo and Ares growled.

"Seriously?" said Cherry. "He's her freaking father, for hell's sake."

River had never heard her mom call Strider that before. But then, she'd never heard her mom call him anything besides Strider. A pang of sadness shot through her, realizing that she'd never called him anything but Strider before either, and he'd been her father for way longer than her actual dad.

Strider walked to where Ares held River and reached out.

Ares looked to River, and she nodded. "It's okay."

He handed her over to Strider, who pulled her against him and kissed her head. “Hey, Kiddo.”

River laid her head on his chest. “Howdy.”

Strider chuckled and, together with Cherry, walked River into the estate.

A scent made River wrinkle her nose. *Vanessa.* She'd been at the estate. The thought made her growl.

"Are you okay, Sweetheart?" he asked.

"I'm fine. Just tired. And tired of being hurt by Titan and his rogues."

He nuzzled her hair, and they followed Cherry up the steps past Zeke and Bianca.

Bianca rushed up to her and kissed River all over the face before swatting her leg and starting to cry.

“Don’t you ever almost die on me again. I need you too much.”

Zeke wrapped his arm around Bianca and gave River a tight smile.

“Don’t blame me,” said River. “You can thank Titan once again.”

"Don't worry," said Cherry. "I'm gonna deal with that piece of shit next."

River was tempted to look over her shoulder to make sure the twins weren't fighting again, but she didn't have the energy to deal with them and her mom.

They were big Alphas. They needed to wear their big wolf pants and stop acting like a couple of adolescent pups. Because if they didn't, she didn't want to be mated to either of them.

CHAPTER THIRTEEN

RIVER

Strider and Cherry took River to her room, and the twins followed closely behind. But when they reached the door, her mom slammed it in their faces.

River groaned. "Mom, you're going to cause an all-out war between them if you don't calm down."

"Me? Me? Why should I calm down? For that matter, why aren't you pissed as hell? They let you get shot, River. I thought I taught you better than that."

River sighed and sank into the large bed. How did she begin to explain to her mom what it was like to be pulled in two different directions by two different men? How the burden of having to choose between them is like asking her to rip part of her soul out and throw it away. How, when she was with Ares, she couldn't think of anything outside of him. And when she was with Apollo, she could see herself raising a family and being happy. Two opposite parts of her life. Both pulling her apart.

"I am pissed," River said. "I'm pissed that I've been put in this position. I'm pissed that I want both of them. I'm pissed my wolf wants both of them. And I'm pissed that I have to choose between them. But there it is. This crapstorm called my life."

Cherry growled. "If you had gone to Jape's like I wanted you to-"

"Then what? I wouldn't have a mate? Children. I'd never feel the touch of a mate truly meant to be mine."

"Trust me, those things aren't everything." Cherry's eyes flicked to Strider, and he walked to the window and looked out. "Just because someone is fated to be your mate doesn't mean they are right for you. Your dad was my fated mate, and my wolf wanted him, which meant I wanted him, but we were never right for each other. And we both knew it. I had my life, he had his, and we both had you. But..." She looked at Strider's back. "Loving someone is different. Yes, most fated mates fall in love and find never-ending joy. However, it's not the case for everyone. Sometimes the one your heart wants and the one your wolf wants are two different people."

A strange sensation rolled over River, and she looked to Strider, who hadn't turned from the window. For the first time, watching her mom watch Strider, she saw it. Love. Her mom loved Strider. Really loved him. She'd never once seen her mom look at her dad like that. But in that moment, River understood. Her dad had been Cherry's fated mate. But Strider had been the one she had chosen before her dad. There was so much she didn't know about them.

"I heard you have to choose between them," her mom said. "I can imagine how hard that is. But my question is, are either of them what you want? I decided to follow what my wolf wanted instead of what I wanted, and the only good thing that came out of it was you. If I knew I could still have you and Bianca, I would have changed my decision."

Cherry's words stunned River. *She* was the only good thing to come out of her mom's mating? If someone ever told her that her mom said that, she never would have believed it.

A knock on the door pulled River's attention. Cherry looked at the door and growled.

River wanted to chastise her mom, but how did you chastise a woman who literally said you were the best thing that had happened to her?

River walked to the door and opened it. Ares stood with Apollo behind him, leaning against the wall across the hallway.

"Hey," said River.

Ares lifted his hand, but looked over her shoulder and dropped it. "The Council would like to speak to you."

"No," said Cherry. "River needs to rest. They can wait."

Ares looked from River to Cherry and back again. "If you would like to wait-"

"Let's get this over with."

River didn't like being summoned like a servant. And even more than that, she didn't like that they summoned her to see if Apollo had been the reason she'd been hurt. So if they wanted to talk, she'd sure as hell talk.

"I'll be back," River said to Cherry. "Do you two have a room?"

Cherry nodded.

"Good. I'll find you in a bit then." River stepped out the door.

"River?" Cherry called.

River looked back.

"Remember who you are."

River nodded. She knew who she was and sure as hell would make sure the Council knew as well.

RIVER ENTERED THE SAME HUGE DINING ROOM SHE HAD DAYS before. The entire scene mimicked the previous one. All Council members sat on one side of the table, and Ares, River, and Apollo took up residence on the other.

Ares and Apollo both pulled out her chair for her, and she sat.

The two groups looked at each other briefly, and then River spoke.

"Why have you summoned me like I'm your assistant?" She couldn't help the annoyance in her voice.

The Council looked at each other and then back at her.

"We heard about your attack, Highness, and we wanted to get some specifics on how that happened," said Osmodius.

"So you thought that gave you the right to order Apollo and me to return here so I could give you a play-by-play of what happened? Why? Are you four the King of the Lycans?"

"No. We are the Council," Osmodius said patiently.

"And that means what? You make the laws?"

"No, we-"

"You enforce the laws?"

"No, we-"

"You rule the Lycans and shifters?"

"No-"

"If you don't do any of those things, who does?"

"The king."

"Right. So Apollo or Ares."

Osmodius's jaw clenched, and then he nodded. "Yes, Highness."

"Do you usually call in Lunas from Lycan packs and ask them how they got hurt? Do you personally oversee every dispute between packs? Call them in over every squabble. Decide on who is at fault?"

"No."

River nodded. "Again, I would like to ask, what gives you the right to summon me to come here and speak to you about anything?"

"Because you are to be the Queen of the Lycans. What happens to you is a matter we all take very seriously."

"Right… so if I were to say… be walking down the stairs with Ares and trip over the carpet and fall and break my leg, I would need to recount that to you?"

Osmodius didn't reply.

"Or if I go out and I'm in a car accident, again, do I need to give you a reenactment? And what if I wasn't driving? Say Bennett's driving. What would happen to him?"

"Your mate would deal with him," said another council member.

"All right. Then why am I conversing with you about it and not my potential mates?"

Osmodius opened his mouth, but River held up her hand to stop him.

"Look. I get it. You guys have been helping run things because there is no crowned king yet. You've given guidance, doled out punishments, and interpreted the laws. But as the future Queen of the Lycans, I'd like to clarify something. I will not, under any circumstances, be beckoned to explain myself by anyone but my mate. If I am injured due to someone else's negligence, I will handle it; if I cannot, my mate will handle it. If I have questions or need guidance, I will go to my mate. If my mate, who will be the King, wants to ask you for guidance, good for him. But for me, I'm me. I will always be me. And I will not be told what to do, where to go, or where to show up by anyone except my mate. If that is a problem for anyone in this room, I suggest you speak now before we go any further."

The Council looked at each other, but no one spoke.

"Good. We all understand that I am not to be treated like a child or a porcelain doll after suffering an almost life-ending injury, having a bullet removed from my shoulder on a kitchen table, and then spending hours in a car uncomfortably trying to get back here to report to you." River nodded. "Now that we have that settled, I have a question for all of you."

"What can we help with, Highness?" asked one of the council members.

River sucked in a deep breath and then clasped her hands in front of her. Her next question wouldn't go over well, but she needed an answer.

"What happens if I can't decide between Apollo and Ares?"

"You have to," said Ares. "You have to choose."

River looked at him. His pained expression made her gut twist.

"But what if I can't? If I won't?"

Anger flashed across Ares' features, and then his gaze saddened.

"You need to decide, Highness," said a council member. "We need a king. We need a queen. We need the royal line to continue."

"Relationships are tenuous at best right now," said Apollo. "A king is needed to reinforce those relationships. To ensure peace between the packs."

"River, this is more than just picking a mate," said Ares. "This is a decision that will affect the future of our societies."

"Exactly," she said. "That's a lot of pressure. I don't know that I can do it."

"You must." Ares pounded his fist on the table.

River jumped to her feet and growled at him.

"River." Apollo took her hand and squeezed it.

She looked at his passive expression.

"Even though I know it might mean I do not get you for myself, Ares is right. You have to choose one of us. Either that or walk away from both of us."

River's heart beat so hard she feared it might give out.

She would have said Ares without a thought if asked to choose four days ago. But now…

She looked between the twins.

She couldn't figure out how to live without either of them.

CHAPTER FOURTEEN

RIVER

River spent the rest of the day in her room, even telling Cherry to leave her alone. River could only take so much of her frantic energy before she snapped, and luckily, Strider saw that point coming and convinced Cherry to go check on Bianca and find food.

The moment they'd left, River locked the door behind them and hid under the covers of the large, soft bed.

For hours, one by one, what seemed like every single person in the estate knocked on her door to try and get her to answer. By the time Bianca made her way to the door, River couldn't hold back the scream that ripped from her. She tried to cover it with a pillow, but she could still hear her little sister's apology and then her footsteps leading away.

It was official. She'd become the Ice Queen from that stupid kid's movie.

River watched the sunset behind the trees surrounding the estate. As her eyelids grew heavy, a click and the sound of something sliding made her eyes pop back open. She looked over to find a prominent figure slithering through her now-open window.

River reached for her knife when a familiar face smiled.

"Hi."

River blew out a harsh breath. "Are you trying to give me a heart attack? I almost threw a knife at you."

"Wouldn't be the first time, Kitten." Apollo chuckled and sat on the inside ledge of the window. "Sorry, but you weren't going to let me in if I knocked again, so I decided I'd better try the other way to ensure you don't starve to death."

Apollo reached out the window and pulled on a rope.

She felt like a kidnapped princess in a tower as he pulled a basket through the window.

"What are you, my Prince Charming?"

"If that's what you want."

River sighed and sat up. "What did you bring as a peace offering?"

Apollo walked to the bed, set the basket down, and let her open it.

She grabbed the soda, cracked it open, and sucked it down. Then she rooted around and fished out a sandwich and a bag of chips.

"What? No prime rib in this place?" she joked.

"I will happily cook you one myself if that's what you want."

She looked at him skeptically. "You cook?"

He shrugged. "Technically, I like to grill and smoke better than cook, but yes, I can."

River bit into the sandwich, not even bothering to see what it was. She shook her head.

"What?"

"I never would have thought the King of the Lycans was a grill master."

"Not all of us like to rely on others to do everything for them."

She looked at him, and he held up his hands.

"Sorry. I know you don't like it when I disparage my brother."

"It's not that I don't like it as much as it's unnecessary. I see both of you how I see you, and talking bad about each other only makes you look bad, not him."

Apollo nodded. "Agreed."

His agreement should have surprised her, but it didn't. Apollo seemed to want to win her over the old-fashioned way, not by trying to make Ares look worse so he would look better. But old habits died slowly, as did old hurts. She couldn't expect him to change overnight.

"So what's been happening out there?"

Apollo shrugged. "Not much. Ares paced in front of your door for about an hour until your mom chased him away, yelling the whole time. Bianca and Zeke tried to calm them both when they got into a yelling match in the dining room. At which point Strider stepped in and got everyone to back off."

"And you did nothing, I suppose."

"Oh no. I stood in the doorway and watched the whole thing. It was quite entertaining until your mom spotted me. I'm smarter than-" he paused. "I'm pretty smart, though, and offered her a beer instead of arguing with her. I'm not sure if she appreciated it or if I just caught her off guard, but she took it from me, downed it, and then walked away."

River chuckled. "Wow. You are smart."

He shrugged. "I try."

Silence fell between them as River finished her sandwich.

"I'm sorry," Apollo finally said.

"Not again."

"No. I'm sorry for everything. All of this. But most of all, I'm sorry I'm too selfish to let you go. I just… can't. You've become everything to me in the few days I've known you. No matter how happy that might make you, I can't give you to Ares."

River set down her can of soda and scooted closer to Apollo. "I am sorry that my indecision is hurting you both. But you have to understand. That feeling you feel for me, I feel that too. I feel it for both of you. I can't explain how or why, but I can, and I do. Which is why I… I can't choose. I can't. I need you both."

She moved until her knees touched his. He looked into her eyes.

"I need you, Apollo. Don't make me choose between you. Please don't." Without thinking, she leaned in and pressed her lips to his.

Apollo hesitated only a moment before he returned her kiss. His tongue swept into her mouth, and she climbed onto his lap and wrapped her good arm around his neck.

Apollo skimmed his hands under the back of her T-shirt, and goosebumps raised on her skin.

She deepened the kiss and moaned as she rocked her hips into his. The contact with her core made her wolf pant. She needed him. All of him. She needed to feel him inside her. To make love to him. Claim him.

"Apollo."

He kissed down her throat, and a slight rumble started in his chest, which relaxed her and drew her in. He kissed her collarbone and kissed across her shoulder.

She winced and pulled back slightly as he got to her injury.

"Sorry-"

She cut off his apology with another kiss. His lips were soft but needy. His kisses passionate and full of promise. River wanted nothing more than to fall into bed with him and feel his mouth touch every inch of her body.

"Apollo, I want you."

"I'm yours, River. Just say the words, and I'll make it permanent here and now."

"I…" She faltered. She did want him. She wanted him to bite her, to take her, to claim her. But she couldn't unless she knew that she could have Ares as well.

"Apollo-"

This time, his lips stopped her from speaking. His hands tangled in her hair, and he flipped over and gently laid her on the bed. His arousal pressed into her core through their clothes, making her want him more than ever.

Making love to him would be just that- making love. Gentle, tender, caring, he would satisfy her every need and desire because it would make her happy and nothing more. She wanted that. She needed that. She needed someone to take care of her, protect her, and make her feel worshiped.

Apollo kissed down her neck and nipped at her breasts through her shirt. His hand slid down between her legs, and she moaned.

"You aren't making this any easier," she panted.

"It's not meant to make things easier. It's meant to help you choose."

River couldn't help the laugh that erupted from her. "I have to admit this is a much better tactic."

He kissed her stomach and raised the hem of her shirt, tickling her side with his breath.

"I'll keep doing it as long as it takes until you make the right choice."

A knock on the door cut off her laugh.

Apollo growled.

"River?" Ares' voice floated through the door. "Are you all right?"

Apollo opened his mouth, but River pressed her hand over it.

"Don't you dare?"

He grinned mischievously and peeled her fingers from his mouth before pressing his lips to hers again.

She kissed him back, her wolf whining for more.

"River?" Ares called again. "Answer me, or I'll break open the door."

Apollo kissed her harder and rubbed between her thighs, making her heat further.

"River-" A crack sounded, and a screech of metal before her bedroom door swung inward.

River broke the kiss with Apollo, and they both stared at Ares as he stood in the doorway. Comprehension dawned on his face, and he roared as he ran to the bed. Apollo jumped up, but River leapt off the bed and between them before the two could come to blows.

She pushed Ares with all her strength. He didn't move backward, but he didn't move forward either.

"No!" she said.

Ares looked down at her.

"Don't."

"I saw him groping you. Kissing you," Ares growled.

"Yeah, and you and I did a hell of a lot more than that," she retorted.

Apollo growled behind her as Ares rested his hand on her waist and squeezed it. His very touch made her wolf roll over and beg for more. Memories of his hands on her in the hotel shower in New York made her skin prickle.

"I'll go," said Apollo. “I need to answer some phone calls anyway, and I have a couple of investment proposals to go over."

River turned, and he kissed her on the head as she gave him a side hug.

"I'll see you later."

Apollo nodded. "Good. Because I have a surprise for you tomorrow."

"A surprise?"

He nodded.

"Tell me."

He chuckled. "Then it wouldn't be a surprise, Kitten. Be patient." Apollo kissed her head again before leaving.

Damn. She wished she could have just five more minutes alone with Apollo. That would be all it would take for her to make him fold like a pup and tell her the surprise.

But that wouldn't happen. At least not right then.

Ares closed the bedroom door, but it swung inward again because he'd broken it. He glanced around and then pushed a massive armoire in front of the door.

"Holy crap, was that necessary?"

Ares rounded on her. "Yes."

The look in his eyes made her body heat.

He strode toward her, his penetrating gaze boring into her and making her wolf roll over in submission.

"Did you let him in?" he demanded.

River's eyes flicked to the window, and Ares' gaze followed hers.

He growled. "Damn, monkey always did like getting around the estate using the roof."

River stared at Ares, his mere presence making her wolf whine.

"Does it bother you he was in here?" she taunted.

Ares strode toward her. She backed up until her knees hit the bed.

He loomed over her and grabbed her hips, pulling them into his. The contact sent shockwaves through her.

"Of course, it bothers me. You're mine. I don't want him anywhere near you."

"And it bothers me that Vanessa was in our house when you told me you sent her away."

Ares nodded. "She just picked up the last few things she'd left behind. I didn't even see her. Zeke let her in. As far as I know, she got her stuff and left."

River's wolf growled.

A smile played on Ares' lips. "Are you jealous, Little Wolf?"

"Jealous, no. Murderous, possibly."

He chuckled. "Then you know how I feel about you with Apollo."

"You know that I'm his, too."

"Not if I can help it." Ares' lips smashed into hers, and just like that, nothing else existed except him.

His tongue probed and claimed her mouth. His strong hands roamed her skin, making her mewl.

He kissed across her chin to her earlobe and bit it.

She grabbed onto him. "Ares," she breathed.

"Yes, Beloved." He bent to his knees and buried his face between her breasts. Lifting her shirt, he exposed her stomach and swirled his tongue across her skin.

She raked her nails through his hair.

He unbuttoned her jeans. "Tell me, you missed me."

River whimpered as he ran his tongue down over her hipbones.

"I… missed you," she choked out.

Ares purred and slid her jeans down over her hips.

Ares never asked what she needed. He just gave it to her and took what he needed in return. It was as if their bodies were one already, and he knew where to touch her to bring her the most pleasure.

He scooped his hands around her hips to her rear and squeezed.

River moaned as her body thrummed. "Ares. I want you."

"I want you too, Beloved." His mouth planted over the apex between her legs, and he teased her through her panties.

"Ares-"

"Say it. Say the words. Choose me. And I promise I will give you everything you've ever wanted and so much more."

He nipped her sensitive nub, and her breath hitched. She couldn't help it. Though she'd been begging Apollo for the same thing only minutes prior, she couldn't help how her body responded to Ares' touch.

"Ares…"

He nipped her again, sending sparks through her legs. "Say it, River. Tell me you want me to claim you. To make you mine forever."

She did. By the goddess, she did. She wanted him more than she'd ever wanted anything… except Apollo. She wanted Apollo just as much. Apollo, with his easy smiles and worshiping kisses. And Ares, with his fiery looks and demanding presence. Two sides to one coin. Total opposites, yet both what she yearned for. City life and country life. Simple yet complicated. Just like she was.

Ares stood, gripped her face, and kissed her hard. She returned his kiss with equal fervor. But as soon as the kiss started, it ended, and he pulled away, leaving her whirling.

Ares stepped back, his eyes black. "You need to decide, River. You can't eat your cake and still have it."

He was teasing her. Taunting her.

Well, she could play just as hard as he could. River shimmied off her jeans and whipped off her shirt, ignoring the scream of her arm.

Ares groaned as she neared him, and the bulge in his pants grew noticeably more prominent.

She pressed her hand to the front of his pants, stroking downward.

His eyes closed, and he sucked in a sharp breath.

She stroked him again and then reached between his legs, grabbed his balls, and squeezed slightly.

He hissed.

She pulled his lips down to hers but stopped an inch away.

"Baby, I don't like cake. I prefer baklava. It has many layers that I can eat one at a time, savoring each one. So that by the time I am done enjoying each gooey, honey-soaked layer, I am thoroughly satisfied."

He leaned in, but River backed away, turned, and crawled under the covers. The sounds of his heavy breathing filled the room.

"Please put the armoire back where you found it before you leave. And make sure someone fixes that door. Who knows who could slip into my room at night and try to take advantage of me with my door broken."

Ares snarled. "Don't worry, Little Wolf. The only one slipping into your room from now on will be me. Anyone else will die."

ARES

Ares closed River's bedroom door, slid off his belt, and wrapped it around both handles, securing them. He looped the belt several more times and then pulled on the end to ensure it couldn't get any tighter.

He stared at the door momentarily, unable to believe he'd had the strength to walk away from her. His mate. His beautiful, curvy, enticing, infuriating mate.

Mine. Take. Mine.

Ares' wolf would not stop screaming at him. Over and over and over. His nails lengthened, and his fangs descended.

Ares grabbed his head. *Shut up! Shut the hell up!*

A chuckle sounded behind him, and Ares whirled around. Apollo leaned against the doorframe of his room, sipping a beer.

"What the hell are you laughing at?"

Apollo snorted. "She told you the same thing, didn't she? That she couldn't choose between us. And now your wolf is going haywire."

Ares took a step forward. "She will choose between us. You better believe she'll choose. I just hope that when she does, you can take the rejection with the grace of a would-be king."

Ares strode past Apollo and down the hallway toward his room.

"And I hope, Brother, that when she chooses me, you will move far away and never bother us again."

Ares stopped. His wolf snarled. He wanted to kill Apollo. Kill Apollo for touching her. For tasting her. For even wanting her in the first place. Apollo the perfect. Apollo, the gentleman. Apollo, the older brother.

Ares clenched his fists. "Believe me, Apollo, if she chooses you, I won't just disappear. You'll never even hear my name whispered again."

Ares stalked to his bedroom and straight into a frigid shower.

CHAPTER FIFTEEN

RIVER

The next day, River felt… strange.

Her warm, sensitive skin didn't even like being touched by the sheets. Her lacy bra felt like sandpaper, so she flung it to the floor. She noticed her suitcases in the corner for the first time and went to them immediately. She found her favorite old Johnny Cash t-shirt and pulled it on. Though it had been her dad's shirt and washed nearly a thousand times, it felt scratchy on her skin. She looked down to find her nipples hard against the fabric.

Great. Just what she needed. She tried pressing on them to get them down, but they didn't. *Wonderful.*

Her stomach growled, and she grabbed it. She looked at the basket of food Apollo brought, but didn't want anything except a second soda.

She crawled to the basket and opened it. She grabbed the soda and sucked it down while looking for something sweet to accompany it. There wasn't anything. She looked through the basket again and then at her bedroom door. She needed food, and she needed it now.

AFTER PULLING ON SOME LEGGINGS, FUZZY SOCKS, AND A PAIR OF slides, River walked to her door and tried the handle. It wouldn't budge. She pulled again, and though the knob turned freely from not having been fixed yet, the doors didn't come apart.

Anger flared, and she banged on the door. "Let me out. Apollo. Ares. What the hell?"

A rush of footsteps and angry voices sounded on the other side of the door before it swung open. She jumped back to keep from being hit by them. Both Apollo and Ares stood in the doorway. Ares held a leather belt in one hand.

She cocked an eyebrow. "Are you going to spank me?"

Ares looked down at the belt and then at her. "I used it to keep the door closed."

Apollo and Ares continued to stare at her, eyes wide.

She looked down at herself. "What? Have you never seen a woman wear a T-shirt, leggings, and fuzzy socks? Do I have to wear a dress or something?"

"Uh…" Ares didn't seem able to form words.

"I think what he's trying to say is, your attire is fine, but maybe you're missing something? Something lacy with cups, perhaps."

River looked at her nipples that were still at attention under her shirt.

"Yeah, that's not happening today. Today is a 'let the ladies fly free' day."

Ares growled.

"Get over it," she said. "They're just nipples. I'm sure you and your men can control yourselves for one day."

Apollo sighed. "I wouldn't be so sure about that."

Ares took his eyes off her for the first time and growled at Apollo. "Stop looking at her."

Apollo cocked an eyebrow. "You stop looking at her."

"No. She's-"

"Your mate? Yeah, we all know that. She's mine too, so I can look at her all I want until she chooses."

Ares' fist tightened around the leather belt, and River thought he might punch Apollo.

"Stop. I'm hot, I'm hungry, and my nipples hurt. So I'm not putting on a bra to make you males feel better. I am going outside to get some fresh air before I suffocate on your toxic masculinity. And I will eat every cinnamon roll, cookie, and bag of candy you have in this place. As well as drink every single soda you possess. Got it?"

They turned back to her.

She shrugged. "What? You've never heard of PMS? I get it, just like every other female. So you should be prepared. In a couple days, I will have cramps that make me want to kill both of you. And I will be eating whatever I want, and neither of you are allowed to say a damn thing about it. We clear?"

They nodded.

"Of course, Beloved."

"Wouldn't dream of it, Kitten."

She sucked in a breath. "Good. Now I want to be shown every gram of sugar in this place."

"As you wish." Apollo smiled. "By the way, if you want to go outside, I can show you your surprise while you're out there."

She'd forgotten about his surprise.

"Don't you need to watch stocks or something?"

He shook his head. "We're good. I'll check on them later. I can field any calls from where we're going."

She smiled. "Then I'm all yours for the day."

Ares' grip tightened further on the leather belt. She ran her hand down his chest.

"Don't worry, Big boy. We'll spend some time together afterward."

"I… have meetings." His gaze flicked to Apollo. "One of us has to keep this place running."

"We divided the duties the way you wanted them divided. I take care of the finances and keep the money flowing, and you take care of the pack business and make sure people don't kill us or each other. If you think I should be doing more, give me more to do," Apollo retorted. "You're the one who always wanted to run everything."

"Because you never do anything but stare at six computer screens and talk on the phone."

River stood between them. "Okay. Okay. That's enough of that." She grabbed Apollo's hand. "Get me some sugar."

Ares laid his hand on her arm. "Dinner at five, and afterward are mine."

She smiled up at him. "Sounds great."

Ares leaned in, sniffed her hair briefly, and then kissed her cheek before Apollo pulled her away.

She couldn't decide if that had gone well as they walked down the hallway toward a back staircase. They'd been in the same room and hadn't threatened to kill or punched each other. River considered it a win.

APOLLO

APOLLO'S WOLF'S JOY AT BEING CHOSEN TO HAVE TIME WITH RIVER first couldn't be described.

Our mate. Our Omega. Ours.

Yes, Apollo assured him. *She is ours.*

Mate. Need.

Apollo sucked in a huge breath and looked over at River. Had she bathed in perfume or something? Her scent seemed more potent, and being near her made his wolf go into a frenzy.

Calm down, bud. Remember the plan. We need to go slow.

No slow. Fast. Need mate now.

Soon. Very soon.

His wolf howled in delight, making Apollo chuckle.

"What's so funny?" she asked as they walked down the stairs toward the kitchen.

"Oh… uh… It's my wolf. He's just happy to be near you."

"Only him, huh?" She cocked an eyebrow at him.

He stopped, and she halted next to him.

"No," he said seriously. "He isn't the only one. You have no idea how little sleep I got last night because I wanted to be near you. To hold you. Touch you. Kiss you. Every time I closed my eyes, you were there. Every breath I took, I smelled you. Every beat of my heart beat only for the purpose of getting me back to you."

Well damn. He hadn't meant for all that to come out of his mouth.

River's eyes sparkled, and she stepped to him and wrapped her arms around his torso. Apollo closed his eyes and pulled her tighter, taking in her sweet scent.

His wolf howled as a ripple of desire traversed his body, making Apollo's pants tighten around his arousal.

Calm down, he told himself. *Calm the freak down before she thinks you want her for nothing more than sex.*

He took several slow breaths, but her scent did nothing to calm him or his wolf. He never wanted to smell anything else for as long as he lived but her scent. He wanted to be surrounded by it. Drowned in it.

A rumble began deep inside and evolved into a mix of purr and growl. She relaxed into him like there was nowhere else in the world she'd rather be.

"Thank you."

Tears moistened his shirt, and he looked down at her, lifting her chin.

"I know I'm not a poet or anything, but I didn't think I was that bad."

She smacked his chest. "You know that's not it." She sniffled twice and wiped at her eyes. "No one's ever said something like that to me before. I just…"

"Just what?"

"Never thought anyone ever would."

"Why?"

She shrugged. "I've never fit in. Not in the human world. Not in the shifter world. And I never once met a guy that felt… right. Then you come along with your sweet words that know where to hit me deep inside to make me…"

His chest squeezed. "Make you what?"

"Make me want to be your mate."

Apollo leaned in and kissed her. "You are my mate, Kitten."

She gripped his shirt and pulled his lips against hers. Apollo's wolf roared inside, and Apollo lifted her off the floor. She wrapped her legs around his waist, and he pressed her into the wall behind them. Her breasts smashed into his chest, and he groaned.

Pressing his weight against her, he reached up and rubbed a thumb over her pert nipple. She gasped and moaned into his mouth. He did it again, and she shuddered at his touch.

She was so warm. So lush. So beautiful. So perfect. He knew then how his father must have felt the moment he'd met his mother. Why his father abandoned Titan's mother as if she had never existed. If River didn't choose him, it wouldn't matter. There would never be another for him. Not ever.

River ground her hips into his and moaned again. She pulled her lips from his and set her head back against the wall, looking into his eyes.

"Apollo..."

The heat radiating from her body and the look in her eyes said it all. She wanted him. And he wanted her.

Take her. Make her ours. Our mate. Our Omega.

Apollo kissed her again and then worked his way down her throat. He slid his hand between their bodies and under her leggings' waistband.

He growled as she gasped and bucked against his fingers as they slid down the inside of her underwear. So wet. So willing.

Apollo's fangs lengthened, and his arms prickled as fur threatened to sprout. He shook as his instincts threatened to overwhelm him and take her right there against the wall in the hallway. Claiming her for himself.

"Apollo-" she gasped.

"I'm sorry," said a voice behind them.

Apollo whipped around, shielding River from view.

Theo.

Apollo's wolf wanted to rip him apart for interrupting them, but he caught himself and stopped just as his nails lengthened.

"I... sorry, Highnesses. I was just... I..." Theo bowed and walked back the way he'd come. "Forgive me."

River giggled behind Apollo, and he turned around. Her cheeks flushed, and her lips were red and swollen from their kisses. Even her hair had been disheveled.

"You think that's funny?" He cocked an eyebrow.

She nodded. "I've never been caught making out with a guy before you. First Lachlan, then Ares, now Theo. I always thought people felt guilty when caught, but I'm sure Theo feels a thousand times worse than I ever will."

Apollo smiled and leaned an elbow on the wall above her head. "Is that so?"

She nodded.

He moved his finger down the front of her shirt, and her breath hitched as he stopped between her breasts.

"I hope you still feel that way, the first time we are walked in on having sex somewhere in the estate."

Her eyebrows shot up. "You think we'll be walked in on somewhere?"

He shrugged. "Seems pretty likely, considering when I make you my mate, I plan on christening every room of this house with you."

Her eyes sparkled, and she smiled. "I like the idea of that."

"Of christening every room?"

"That, and someone walking in on us."

Apollo growled. "I'll get mirrors put above our bed, Kitten.

Because yours are the only eyes I won't rip out if someone watches me make love to you."

He swooped in and kissed her hard. She moaned and bit his bottom lip.

Apollo's body shook as his instincts took over once more.

Instead, he stepped away and took her hand. "Come on. Let's get you that sugar overload you need, and then I can show you your surprise."

She pouted for a fraction of a second and then fell in step next to him. "If the surprise isn't you on my bed with a can of whipped cream in one hand and a jar of sprinkles in the other, I'm pretty sure I'm going to be disappointed.

Apollo burst out laughing and put an arm around her shoulders, kissing the top of her head. "Oh, River, you are quite perfect."

As Apollo and River walked into the kitchen, everything went silent. Apollo scanned the large area where the three cooks stood, already preparing food. At a table usually reserved for the cooks to eat, Cherry, Strider, Bianca, and Zeke sat, sharing a meal.

Cherry stood when they entered. "Did you wake her up?"

Apollo sighed inwardly and planted a smile on his face. He reminded himself that Cherry might be a bit aggressive and brash, but she cared about River- even if she didn't show it in the ways mothers normally did.

"No. I got up on my own. I'm a big girl like that."

Cherry didn't even bite at River's snarky reply. "Show me your wound."

River rolled her eyes, and Apollo held back a smirk.

"I just told you I'm a big girl."

"Show me." Cherry's gaze hardened, and she continued to stare at River.

"Fine." River pulled her shirt to the side. "Happy?"

Cherry's gaze flicked to Apollo. "No. I am not happy. I'm not happy you're here. I'm not happy you were shot. I'm not happy-"

River held up her hands. "I get it. You aren't happy. What else is new?"

Cherry pulled the neck of River's T-shirt down, then stepped back and looked at her. "Are you not wearing a bra?"

River swallowed and folded her arms across her chest. "No. I'm not if you must know."

Cherry sniffed her, and her eyes narrowed before she looked at Apollo.

After a minute, River grabbed her arm. "Stop that. Leave him alone."

Cherry growled and pulled away. "You're Apollo, right?"

Apollo nodded.

Cherry sniffed and walked away without another word. She retook the chair next to Strider, and he whispered something in her ear. Apollo swore for a fraction of a second the corner of Cherry's lips quirked upward.

Interesting. So, she did have a soft spot.

Bianca got up from the table and rushed to River, flinging her arms around her. "Oh my gosh, River. I've been a mess. We get here, and you've gone away, and I'm going crazy not knowing where you are or what you are doing, and then you get shot, and no one would let me see you."

River grabbed onto her sister and hugged her. "It's okay, B. I'm here. I'm fine. I'm sorry I screamed at you."

For the next several minutes, River continued to console her sister, as if Bianca had been put through a terrible ordeal, not River.

Zeke stood and peeled Bianca off River. Bianca turned and clung to Zeke instead.

Zeke met Apollo's eye and bowed his head. "Highness."

Apollo held out his hand. Zeke looked at it, and he could swear he heard River gasp.

Zeke shook Apollo's hand.

"Apollo. Just Apollo. No need to be so formal anymore if we are going to be related."

Apollo could see the wheels turning in Zeke's head. If River chose Apollo, what would that mean for him and his mate? They would be related through marriage, but he was still Ares' bodyguard and friend.

"Thank you, Highness," Zeke replied.

Apollo never disliked Zeke. He was a solid guy. Good at his job and loyal. Unlike Theo and Santiago, who, to be honest, Apollo had always been jealous of because they were so close to Ares. For years, he'd wished it had been him. However, that dream had long since died.

River smiled and slipped her hand into his again.

Apollo winked.

Cherry motioned them over. "Eat. Get your strength back."

"River just came to raid our pantry for sweets and soda," said Apollo.

Bianca giggled. "Oh man, River's infamous PMS is striking. Growing up, we had an entire cabinet dedicated to River's PMS week."

"We did not," said River.

"Yes, we did," Cherry replied. "Six full shelves stocked with every sugary item we could buy."

River huffed. "You guys ate that stuff too."

"Sorry, Sweetheart," said Strider. "It was all for you. We kept our sweets locked in our rooms for safekeeping."

River's cheeks deepened to a beautiful shade of pink. She opened her mouth and then closed it again.

"Come on," said Apollo. "Let's go create your private shelf in the pantry."

She elbowed him and pulled her hand away. "You are so funny."

He chuckled. "Usually." He retook her hand and led her toward the pantry.

Embarrassment still wafted off her as she mumbled about not eating that much candy.

RIVER

RIVER COULDN'T BELIEVE THE EMBARRASSMENT SHE ENDURED AT HER family's hands in front of Apollo. Okay, so she liked her sweets. It wasn't like she was shooting cola or anything. However, she had snorted Pixie Stix once. That had been painful.

Apollo carried a bag of goodies for her as he led her out of the back of the estate and onto the back lawn.

"Where's my fudge?" she asked.

"What?"

"My fudge. And my bag of candy. I never did get those back when we were at the cabin."

Apollo's eyes narrowed. "You know, I never got mine back either."

She snorted. "Well, from how I saw the guys digging into your bag after they took it from you, I'm not surprised. But I am surprised they ate mine."

"They wouldn't dare. I'll be sure to find it for you tonight."

She smiled. "You better, or I'm going to make them go back and get me more."

He nodded. "I'll make them walk to get it."

"Nah. That would take too long."

"True."

A huge fountain took up residence just beyond an expansive patio that wrapped around the entire back of the estate. As they walked down the stone steps and passed the fountain, she noted several enormous koi fish swimming inside it.

"Don't they freeze in the winter here?"

"No. We keep it heated for them all year into the fall, but when it gets too cold, we have a room inside with a large tank that they are moved to."

It surprised her that they took so much care of fish.

They walked beyond the fountain and down toward a large pool.

"Do you ever use the pool?"

"Me? No. Ares does occasionally. Mostly, we kept it because my parents used to have large parties back when they were alive, and the pack leaders loved the pool."

"Maybe it will be that way again once there is a king."

"Maybe. Though I can't see Ares holding pool parties."

River looked up at Apollo. It struck her that Apollo thought Ares would be the next king and not himself.

They headed through rows of flowerbeds toward a building near the back of the lawn.

"Where are we going?" she asked.

"Why? Is having to wait to scarf down all your sweets making you cranky?"

She shoved him.

"We are going to that old barn."

"Do we have cows to milk?"

"Not exactly." A sly smirk spread across his face.

"What are you up to?"

"We'll be there in a minute."

She sighed.

"Trust me. I am sure you'll like this surprise." He raised her hand and kissed her knuckles.

The brush of his lips on her skin made her flush with warmth, and her heartbeat quicken.

He paused and looked at her. There was no use trying to hide her reaction. He was more than capable of reading her… everything.

He smiled and continued to lead her across the lawn.

"So, I'm surprised I haven't even thought to ask this before, but what is the difference between Lycans and shifters? You are stronger, faster, larger, quicker to lose your temper."

"I prefer to think of us as more hot-blooded instead of just angrier."

She smiled. "But what else? I mean, can you smell stronger or see farther?"

"Probably."

"How do you know?"

He pulled her to a stop. "Because when I do this." He kissed her hand again. "I notice the slight sweetness that comes into your scent. And when I do this." He wrapped an arm around her waist and brought her body into full contact with his. He leaned into her ear. "Your heart beats ten times faster. And when I do this." He squeezed her rear. "Your skin heats by at least a degree."

She pushed him away. “Those are things I could tell about you as well. Your scent is always prevalent. Smoky and woodsy. And I bet I don't even need to touch you to make your heart beat faster.”

"You think so, do you?"

She nodded. "I know so."

"You're pretty full of yourself."

River grinned and bent her knees until she knelt on the ground before him.

"What are you doing?"

"Nothing."

She inched closer to him until her breath hit the crotch of his jeans.

She didn't need to be a shifter to feel the tension in his body ratchet up.

"River." He looked around. "People could be watching."

She moved even closer until her face was inches from his ever-growing erection.

"River-"

She looked up at him and grinned. "Told you I didn't need to touch you to make your heart beat faster. You just heated up by a couple of degrees, too."

She jumped to her feet and laughed at the expression on his face. He looked like he wanted to kiss her and eat her at the same time.

His hands clenched and unclenched rapidly, and then he shook his head.

"I take it my surprise is in that barn." She motioned with her head.

Apollo didn't speak, only nodded.

"Great. Bring my sugar buffet."

She turned and walked toward the barn. Her wolf grumbled.

What's your problem?

Games. Don't like it.

River rolled her eyes. *Please. It's no different than when you ran with his wolf in the woods.*

She neared the barn and realized Apollo still stood where she'd left him, staring at the sky.

"Hey, you coming?" she called.

"Almost," he replied without looking at her.

She laughed. "Hurry up. I want my surprise!"

River jogged forward to the door and threw it open just as Apollo said, "Wait."

She took in the space, and her jaw dropped.

Apollo came to a stop beside her. "Do you ever listen?"

She stared into the open space, and her chest squeezed. On one wall hung every tool she could think of for carving wood. It had to be thousands, if not tens of thousands, of dollars' worth of tools. The piece of wood she'd been carving with Walt stood in the middle of the floor.

"I thought you could use this half of the bottom floor for woodworking and the other side for your metalwork. Upstairs-"

River didn't let him finish. Instead, she grabbed him and pulled his lips to hers. He dropped the bag of sugary goodies and threaded his hands into her hair.

She lost time kissing him. And pulled away only because her stomach growled.

He chuckled. "Sugar over sexy stuff. Noted."

She looked at him thoughtfully. "Thank you, Apollo. I… thank you."

He brushed a hair from her eyes and kissed her again. "You are very welcome, River."

She reached up on her toes, rubbed her nose on his, and then backed up. The look that crossed his face made her think he might cry. He pulled her to him and pressed her into his chest.

She wrapped her arms around him and smiled. This. This is what she wanted, what she'd hoped for in a mate. After a minute, he let go of her, and she peered up at him.

"Can I?"

"Why do you think I brought you out here?"

She yipped with delight, raced to the piece of wood, and ran her fingers over it, remembering where she'd left off days before.

"I'm gonna bring a table down from upstairs and set all your goodies out."

She nodded and continued to feel the wood. Then she went to the wall and pulled down a small chainsaw. Most of the big carving was done, so it was time to start on the finer details.

River tied her hair up in a ponytail and revved the chainsaw. The smell of the motor oil made her smile. Memories of her dad came back to her, and her eyes misted.

She looked around the barn as Apollo returned with a circular table. Her chest squeezed at the sight of him, and her wolf chuffed.

Home.

Yeah, said River. We're *home.*

CHAPTER SIXTEEN

APOLLO

Apollo stared at River, chisel in her hand and a Twizzler hanging out of her mouth, working meticulously on her carving. She stepped back and wiped at the piece, chewed the licorice into her mouth, and finished it.

In the hours that they'd been in the barn, she'd finished off two packs of Twizzlers, a bag of chocolate, a bag of circus peanuts, a container of cotton candy, two large oatmeal cookies, and a six-pack of cola. He had no idea how she wasn't bouncing off the walls. Or throwing up. Just one more of the mysteries that made up River.

She walked to the wall and put the chisel back. Then, she grabbed a small Dremel tool and went toward the wood, but stopped and walked to him instead.

"Aren't you bored?"

Apollo picked several flecks of wood shavings out of her hair. "Nope."

"I would be going crazy just sitting here the way you have."

"Especially if you'd eaten all that sugar."

She looked at the table. "I overdid it, didn't I?"

He shrugged. "Just wait until you see me at an all-you-can-eat Chinese buffet."

"Were you able to get any work done with the noisy chainsaw and tools?"

Apollo nodded. "I put off the calls I could until later and did a lot through text. I've never been a fan of texting before, but I feel it will be quite helpful moving forward."

She snorted, "Well, I hope we don't become one of those couples who go out together, but sit on our phones and text other people."

Apollo chuckled. "Kitten, when we are out together, you will have my undivided attention every second. So much that you will get sick of me. If you want to go out now, I can prove it."

"Sure, I-" Her eyes widened. "What time is it?"

Apollo looked at his phone. "Five thirty."

"Shit!"

Just then, the door to the barn cracked open, and Ares stormed in, eyes icy and body rigid.

"Ares-" River headed toward him.

"I should have known you'd do this." He strode toward Apollo. "All day. I gave you all day with her, and even that wasn't enough. You had to ruin the evening for me as well."

He stopped feet from Apollo, and River stepped between them.

"Ares. It's not like that. It's not-"

"His fault? Of course not. It's never Apollo's fault."

Apollo ground his teeth together, biting back the words that popped into his head.

"Ares. I'm serious. It's not about fault. I lost track of time. That's all."

Ares snorted, but his eyes stayed on Apollo. "Stop making excuses for him."

"Stop being an ass and listen to me," River demanded.

Ares' gaze moved to River, and the shift in Ares' posture surprised Apollo.

River reached for Ares' hand. "Look what I did, and you'll understand."

Ares' body relaxed further. He looked at Apollo and then at River again.

"Show me."

River smiled and pulled him over to her sculpture.

Apollo swallowed hard, and his wolf snarled. The barn was a gift he'd given River. He didn't like that she showed it to Ares. For the hours she'd sculpted, it felt like the barn might turn into their place.

She showed Ares the wolf sculpture. He put his arm around her waist, and Apollo's wolf leapt to his feet, ears flat and hackles raised.

Apollo's chest squeezed, and he turned to the door. His time was up. He'd had her all day. He had to honor her wishes to spend the rest of the evening with Ares. He just hoped that the evening didn't turn into her spending the whole night with him.

ARES

ARES KNEW THE MOMENT APOLLO LEFT. THOUGH HIS ENTIRE BODY was in tune with River's, the presence of his twin always had him on edge.

Sadness and rage swirled inside him. His. She was his. She was everything to him. His heart pounded. He'd initially begun to panic when he'd not found her inside the house, but Theo told him he'd seen them heading to the old barn. He couldn't have imagined why they'd gone out there, but the moment he'd opened the door, his heart had sunk.

Apollo made her a space to create. The realization almost brought Ares to his knees. He should have thought of it. Hell, he'd had days without her. He should have spent every moment making the estate how she would like it, but Apollo had again outdone him. The notion that Apollo might take her from him made him want to die. And if he did take her… Ares knew he'd wish he were dead. He hadn't been kidding when he'd told Apollo that if he didn't get River, he would do more than disappear.

The idea made his wolf growl.

River pulled him around the sculpture, showing him different techniques she'd used, and with every smile, every glance his way, his anger abated, and his wolf backed down.

"I didn't know you worked with wood. I thought you just did metal."

"When I was with Apollo, we went to town, and a chainsaw carver was there. I started this piece there. I didn't know Apollo brought it back."

"So Apollo made this for you. This workshop."

River glared at him for a moment and then put her hands deep in his suit pants pockets, making him harden.

"He did. But you can have your own side."

"What do you mean?"

"There's a whole other side over there I could use for metal working. I brought my favorite tools, but I'll need others. You can put those things over there, and that will be our side."

Ares wolf growled. "You mean there will be a side for him and then a side for me?"

"Yup."

Ares blew out a harsh breath. "River-"

She pressed her fingers to his mouth. "Don't. Don't tell me I have to choose. Don't ruin our time together. Let's just be together. You and me."

He brushed flakes off her shirt. "You and me." *The way it should be.*

For the first time, he wished that they'd stayed in New York. That they'd waited to come back. If he'd just been more patient and less paranoid, she would have bonded to him exclusively, and they'd be mated already, and there would be nothing Apollo could do about it.

So many things he wished he could change. But it was too late.

Ares noticed her breasts bounced a bit more than usual. "Why aren't you wearing a bra today?"

"I told you about my nipples, but… that wasn't the whole truth."

"Tell me."

"I've been feeling weird. I woke up hot and sensitive, so I chose not to wear one. Oh, and I ate my weight in sugar as well."

She did feel slightly warmer than usual. Worry rooted in his gut. "You aren't getting sick, are you?"

She shook her head. "Guess PMS is just hitting harder than usual."

He sniffed her. Even her scent was more aromatic. "Are you sure you're okay? If you aren't feeling well, we can stay in so you can rest. I know you've been through a lot."

She touched his face. "I'm fine. Trust me, if I felt sick, I would tell you."

He searched her face, but she didn't appear to be lying.

She kissed his cheek. "I promise. I'm okay."

Ares nodded but could not get rid of the feeling that something was different.

She stepped forward and pressed against him. "How about a shower, and then we get food?"

His blood heated. "I like that idea. We can use my shower. It's bigger."

She laughed. "I meant I would shower."

"I don't mind helping you get clean. As I remember, we are pretty good at helping each other."

He remembered the feel of her in the shower. Her curvy body, hard and soft at the same time, and perfectly molded to his.

She smiled, and he caught the slight flush on her cheeks. "As much as I enjoyed that, I am pretty hungry, and I get the feeling that if we start something now, there will be no stopping until morning."

Ares groaned. Damn, having her in his shower, his bed, on the floor, and in front of his fireplace all sounded terrific.

"I'm okay with that."

She reached up on her toes and kissed him lightly. "Shower."

He bent down and nuzzled her neck. "I like how you smell."

"You like the smell of motor oil and wood?"

"No. I like how *you* smell. You smell like cherries and vanilla, only stronger, sexier. It usually drives me crazy, but right now...

Right now, it is taking everything inside me not to devour you on the spot."

He nipped her neck.

She giggled.

"Makes me want to lick every inch of you. To suck your fingers into my mouth, one by one, and move my way down to taste every delicious inch of you."

Her body quivered, and his wolf howled in delight.

More. Mate. Now.

Ares swirled his tongue over her collarbone, and her fingers dug deep into his shirt.

"Ares," she breathed.

"River."

He kissed her skin, making her pant and pull him closer.

Ares wolf howled. *Claim. Mate. My Omega.*

He claimed her mouth with his, and she attacked him. Her lips and tongue were hot and needy on his as her breasts smashed against him, making him want to strip off his clothes and be skin-to-skin with her.

She mewled, and her hands found his rear. Ares' fangs dropped into his mouth.

Bite her. Take her.

His wolf strained against his tether, and Ares stepped away before his restraints broke.

No!

She looked at him, confused. "What's wrong?"

Ares sucked in several sharp breaths. "My wolf… wants you."

His nails lengthened, and she stepped toward him, but he held up his hand, and she stopped.

Back down, you idiot, or we'll lose her.

His wolf paced and snapped, but Ares forced him to submit.

"Are you okay?"

He swallowed hard and then straightened. "Yeah. It's just... getting more difficult to hold him back."

Concern etched her features.

"I won't hurt you, River. And I won't take you without you choosing me."

She moved forward and cupped his cheek. "I know you won't, my Alpha. I trust you. I'm worried about you."

His chest squeezed at her words. "Don't. I'm more stubborn than my beast."

She stepped to him and laced her fingers in his. "I don't want you to be stubborn. I want you to be happy. And I know all of this, on top of all you deal with, has to be pushing you and your wolf to the brink."

He stared down into her beautiful face. "No matter what happens, as long as you are by my side, I can get through anything."

"And I with you."

He'd never been good with words. Action was his domain. Even so, he wanted to tell her. To help her understand just what she meant to him. What he was prepared to do to have her as his mate.

"You tell me, Beloved. Tell me right now to mark you, and I'll forget all the plans I've made for the next six months just to stay in bed with you. You tell me to give up the throne and move back to New York, and I won't even pack. You say you want to live on a deserted island with no cell service, and I'll drop my phone in the fountain outside, and we'll be on a plane in twenty minutes. Anything you want, you say the word, and I'll give it to you.

Nothing in my life has ever meant to me what you do." He held his breath, waiting, praying for her to say the words.

Instead, she shook her head. "I would never ask that of you."

"But you could, and I'd do it."

"And knowing that makes me feel terrible. Terrible because I want to say those things. I want to tell you to claim me and make me yours, because I am already yours. Every fiber of who I am is yours. But I'm also his. Can you do that for me? Can you share me?"

Ares growled, but even as he did, he thought about it. Could he? Could he share her if I meant he'd lose her? Was part of her better than none of her? As much as he hated to admit it, he already knew he would be willing to take whatever she wanted to give him. Every moment. Every touch. Every everything. If he had to decide between sharing and not keeping her, he'd do what he had to.

River kissed him and walked toward the door. "Are you coming?"

"You gonna let me watch?"

She snorted. "No. But I'll let you pick out what I wear."

It was not even close to what Ares wanted, but he'd take it. "Good, because I already bought you a dress."

Her eyes lit up. "You did? Does that mean we're going somewhere nice?"

He smiled. "It's a surprise."

She rolled her eyes. "You Alphas and your surprises. One of these days, I'm going to do something for you and call it a surprise, and then I'm going to make you wait a whole week before I tell you what it is."

He chuckled. "Believe me, Sweetheart, you wouldn't last a week."

Her eyes sparkled. "Challenge accepted."

She walked out the door, and Ares looked at the wood carving again. As beautiful as it was, it made him frown. The wolf looked identical to Apollo's.

CHAPTER SEVENTEEN

RIVER

The SUV stopped on a busy street, and River looked around at the bustle of the evening.

"Where are we going?" she asked.

Ares smiled. "I thought that since this will be your new home, you might appreciate seeing some of Montreal's beautiful things. We won't go out every night, but the city has some amazing sites."

That wasn't an answer, but like his brother, Ares didn't like to give up his surprise until the last minute. She made a note to be true to her word and figure out a surprise for both brothers that she wouldn't tell them for at least a week.

Theo rolled down the driver's side window and spoke to a policeman on the street. The man nodded and showed Theo down to a private parking spot. They parked, and Drew pulled up the second SUV right behind them. Ares hopped from his side of the vehicle and walked around to her side. He buttoned his suit jacket and then opened her door for her.

River's dress rode up her thigh as she stepped out in the heels Ares picked for her. She tipped sideways only a fraction before Ares wrapped his arm around her, steadying her. Her cheeks heated, but she still didn't have the guts to tell him she'd only worn heels on two previous occasions. Once, when her cousin had mated, and River had been part of the ceremony, and the second time at her show a few weeks prior.

"Damn, have I told you how good you smell today?"

"Only a couple times." She shook her head. "Have I told you how sexy you are in a suit?"

Ares growled and nipped her neck. "I wish you had let me shower with you."

She kissed his cheek. "But then you wouldn't have taken me to see what the city has to offer."

"Trust me, I can offer more than the whole city from the comfort of my bed."

She snorted. "You are so cocky."

"Only for you."

Ares straightened and nodded to Theo and Santiago, who led the way. They exited the private parking area and emerged onto a crowded street. A wave of fear washed over River as she realized she was in a city of strangers, in a foreign country, and had no way of getting anywhere if something happened.

Ares pulled her closer. "Don't worry. I won't let anything happen to you. Just like in New York."

She heard the words he didn't say- *Like Apollo had.*

She took a breath and nodded.

Ares ushered her forward with Theo and Santiago out front and

Zeke and Lachlan behind. The wall of black suits and gigantic men made River feel safer, but also blind. Though she could see the occasional person snapping photos of the strange group, she could see nothing else.

After about a block, they came into a brightly lit area.

Theo stopped. "I'll get your food. Santiago, take them to the *La Grande Roue de Montréal* and get them seated, and I'll be along shortly."

Theo peeled to the right as Santiago led them forward. With half her shifter wall having walked away, River could finally see where they were headed.

Her stomach flopped. "I'm not getting on that thing."

Ares chuckled. "We will be in a private gondola. It is enclosed in glass and will take us up slowly to the top."

"Yeah, and then it comes back down over and over."

He squeezed her hand. "No, it won't. I bought all the tickets. We have the whole thing to ourselves for the next hour. Trust me, once you see the sunset from the top of *La Grande Roue,* you will never see it the same way again."

River looked at him dubiously.

Ares leaned in and whispered. "If you get scared, you can sit on my lap."

She narrowed her eyes. "Is that the real reason you brought me here? To get me on your lap?"

He smiled. "I am pretty sure I could have thought of a lot easier way of getting you on my lap."

True.

Her wolf chuffed.

They approached the wheel, and the man bowed and opened the door to a glass-encased gondola. River swallowed hard but had to admit it looked pretty safe inside. There were four leather seats. Little tables. And warm air wafted out.

She hesitated and thought about begging Ares not to make her go, but what kind of Omega would she be if she let a little Ferris wheel scare her? She looked up. Okay, a huge Ferris wheel.

"If you don't like it, we will come back down. All right?"

She swallowed hard and nodded, trying to keep from screaming and running away.

Ares helped her in, then ducked and followed her. The gondola swayed slightly, and River sat in the nearest seat.

Ares chuckled and sat across from her.

She blew out a breath and rubbed her palms on her short dress.

The minute Theo showed up with the bags of food, River grabbed the soda from him and sucked it down.

"Thank you," said Ares.

Theo nodded and closed the door. Outside, he said something to Drew and Lachlan, then nodded to the operator.

River closed her eyes and pressed her palms into the seat armrests. As the wheel moved backward, she groaned.

Ares sat forward and took her hands in his. She squeezed his hands tight.

"Hey."

She couldn't reply.

"Look at me."

She blew out a breath and opened her eyes. He leaned in and kissed the knuckles on both hands.

"Just keep your eyes on me."

She nodded as her throat tightened.

"I promise. This might seem scary, but you are going to love it."

She nodded again, trying to force her muscles to relax.

"I was five the first time I came here," he said. "My parents brought Apollo and me downtown for the Christmas season to shop. I saw this giant wheel and wanted nothing more than to go on it."

"And that's when you fell in love with it?"

He snorted. "Uh… not exactly. I started to freak out the minute we got inside. Apollo just sat there staring out the window like it was nothing. But I almost pissed myself."

She couldn't imagine Ares being scared. "What happened?"

"My mother cradled my head in her lap while I cried the entire time and refused to look out the window. And then the minute we got off the ride, I vomited all over my mom's shoes."

River couldn't help but laugh.

"After that, my father brought me every year at Christmas. Just him and me alone. He would get us a gondola and make me look out the window. He would talk to me and hold my hand. He talked about his life. My mother. Being King. He asked what I wanted from life. What I saw myself doing in the future. And most of all, he talked to me about what it would be like when I found my mate. How to treat her and give her everything she ever wanted. It was my favorite day of the year growing up. I looked forward to it all year long. It was the only time I ever got him all to myself. He spent so much time with Apollo that I cherished our hours together. By the time I was ten, I wasn't scared anymore, but I pretended I still was just so my dad would bring me."

River looked into his eyes and saw the pain in them. "You miss him, don't you?"

Ares nodded. "More than you can know."

She gave a sad smile. "I do know."

He stared at her, and they shared a moment of pain from the loss of their fathers. But he was right. As much as she missed her dad, Strider had stepped up and been everything she could have asked for in a stepfather. Ares and Apollo hadn't gotten that.

The wheel slowed, and River glanced out the window at the sunset before returning to Ares.

"He sounds like a great man."

"He was. Strong. Smart. He was kind but ruthless when necessary. I heard he was not known for kindness before meeting my mother. But I never knew that man. I only knew the man he was because of my mother. And that's what I want. I want to be a man like he was."

River reached up and cupped his cheek. "You will be."

He leaned into her palm and closed his eyes. "You make me want to be that man, River."

Her chest squeezed. They sat that way for a minute, and then he opened his eyes.

"Let's eat. We only have about forty-five minutes before we need to leave."

"Is there somewhere else we need to be?"

He nodded.

She sighed. "Let me guess, another surprise?"

He chuckled.

She shook her head. "You know, I'm going to be very happy when I know what my schedule is for the day instead of having everything sprung on me at the last minute."

"Trust me, Beloved. I will never stop surprising you. I will never stop taking you to experience new things. And I will never let a day go by that something magical doesn't happen for you."

She squeezed his knee. "Ares, you don't have to do that."

He nodded. "I know, but that's the thing. I want to. Making you happy is the only thing I want out of life. You and our children are more important to me than anything. Nothing else. Nothing. You are all I want."

River's chest squeezed, and tears filled her eyes. *Damn Lycans.*

"And you are who I want. Even if that means I have to deal with bodyguards, people not saying my name, a Council who thinks they can tell me what to do, a huge house I will never clean, and dressing in high heels to please you. Though at some point, I will most likely break an ankle."

He kissed her gently, opened the bags of food, and pulled out two sandwiches. "Grilled cheese or turkey?"

She smiled. "Which one do you want?"

"The one you don't."

"We're going to starve to death playing this game. Which one do you want?"

He looked at the sandwiches. "Turkey."

"Then I will have the grilled cheese. See, making magical things happen every day goes both ways."

His face changed in that moment, and when he smiled, River saw the true Ares.

AFTER EATING SANDWICHES, A PLETHORA OF PASTRIES AND CAKE, AND drinking the best-tasting wine she'd ever had, they rotated back to the ground, where Lachlan opened the door, and the guards walked them back to their SUV.

"Where next?"

Ares kissed her head, and she rolled her eyes.

"You know I'm going to plan a great big surprise for you when we get home, and you will hate it so much that you will stop trying to surprise me."

Ares chuckled. “You keep saying that.”

Just when she was about to question him further, the car stopped, and River spotted a large cathedral on the right.

She laughed and looked at Ares. "You're taking me to church? Should I be wearing a white dress? I didn't even know you were Catholic."

Ares got out of the vehicle, and like before, he opened the door for her and helped her out. He held her hand and walked her up the sidewalk.

"Yes, I am taking you to a church. No, I am not Catholic. But you don't have to be a Catholic to enjoy what we are about to see."

She looked at him quizzically and continued forward through the crowd. They reached the cathedral's entrance, and Santiago handed over six tickets. The man at the door took them and motioned for them to enter. River's eyes widened at the sight. The inside of the cathedral was like nothing she'd ever seen. Stained glass, tall statues, and candles adorned the building everywhere she looked. The ceiling joists alone left her breathless. She stood in awe, taking it all in and relishing the beauty and craftsmanship of the building.

"Do you like it?" Ares whispered.

"It's breathtaking. Did you make it?"

He snorted before smacking her rear. "Smart ass. Let's get some seats."

Santiago and Drew went in first, followed by River and Ares. Lachlan and Zeke brought up the rear. They located seats in the second row and sat.

River didn't like the idea of taking Zeke from Bianca just so he could guard her, but she reminded herself it was his job. And he wasn't just watching after her; he watched over the possible next king of the Lycans. But as soon as they were all mated, she planned on talking to Ares about letting Zeke and Bianca come with them to things like this as a couple. As well as the other mates of his men.

For several minutes, River continued to look around, and then the lights in the cathedral dimmed, and music started. She shivered as her body cooled, but felt too warm at the same time. *Damn.* She hoped she wasn't coming down with something. Nothing was worse than being sick and on your period.

FOR THE NEXT FIFTY MINUTES, SHE WATCHED WHAT COULD ONLY BE described as Monet meeting Beethoven. Lights flickered, sprouting colors all over the walls and ceilings. Gorgeous hues of blues, greens, and purples bathed every surface. It was like an indoor firework show set to medieval chamber music and Renaissance paintings. It both dazzled and took her breath away.

The only thing that detracted from the performance was how her clothes felt too constricting, and her dress began to irritate her skin. She wished Ares had opted for a backless dress or something similar, so she wouldn't have had to wear a bra. She took to fanning herself with a piece of paper she'd found in her purse, but she was sweating anyway.

After the show, she pulled Ares in and kissed him until she was breathless.

"If that's what I get for showing you a church, I wonder what taking you to a royal palace would get me."

She smiled. "This was amazing. I… I have no words."

"That may be a first."

She shook her head. "Way to ruin a moment."

"If I kiss you again, will the moment start over?"

"Maybe."

Ares' gaze intensified, and then he laced his fingers at the base of her neck and pulled her lips to his again. He started soft, but soon his lips claimed hers, and his tongue probed her mouth, wanting more.

Minutes passed, and he pulled away.

"You smell amazing. I've missed you, Beloved."

She touched his face. "Me too."

Ares' eyebrows scrunched for a moment, and he held her palm against his face and sniffed it.

"Your skin is almost hot."

"Maybe that's just because you are so hot that being near you rubs off on me," she teased.

His eyes darkened, but then Zeke interrupted them. "Highness, most of the place is cleared out. Should I get the car?"

Ares nodded. "Yes."

Until that moment, River hadn't noticed that the guards had surrounded them, shielding them from every angle.

"Can I go see the front?"

"Of course."

Ares took her hand and led her to the front of the basilica, where hundreds of candles flickered in glass jars. She looked at the statues behind the altar. Although she had never been religious, she could appreciate both the beauty of the statues and the effort that went into creating them. In the middle, the crucifixion of Christ was framed by four statues on either side. The apostles, she guessed. There were further statues even higher up. Gothic woodwork and metalwork framed the entire space. Gorgeous gold foiled pillars in deep blues and reds were stunning to behold. She imagined bending the metal and the wood to the shapes she wanted to achieve the gothic aesthetic. Pointed, round, beautiful, perfect. She'd never been able to paint or draw like the beautiful scrollwork done in the cathedral, but she sure would like to take a crack at possibly making a stained-glass window sometime.

River didn't know how long she studied the structure before Ares' phone buzzed. She looked at him, and he nodded to Santiago.

"Car is out front. We can stay longer if you want, though."

She wanted to stay forever, but in a rush, fatigue washed over her, and she shivered.

"No, that's okay. But I would like to come back in the daytime and see it in the light."

"We can do that whenever you want."

She snuggled into his side, and they walked down the aisle to the exit. She wished she could do something for Ares. For Ares and Apollo. They'd both done so much for her, given so much for her. She wished she could return the favor, but had no idea how.

As they stepped out into the chilly night air, Ares immediately removed his jacket and put it around her shoulders.

"You'll get cold," she protested.

"Nonsense. I'm used to the cold of Montreal. You, however, aren't yet. Besides, we are only going a hundred feet to the vehicle. And you can't hide the fact that you've shivered at least a dozen times inside the building, but your skin is still warmer than it should be. You are getting sick."

She gave him a weak smile. "I think it's just exhaustion. Coming to Canada, going to the woods, the shooting, and then working all day today. I think I overdid it a bit, is all."

"I didn't realize that shifters got sick."

"It's rare, but we do. Don't you?"

"No. Our metabolism burns everything out too fast."

His eyes held concern, but she took his hand, and he walked her to the SUV.

As soon as they slid into the backseat, River snuggled into Ares' arms and closed her eyes.

"Thank you for tonight," she said.

"You are most welcome."

"Did you enjoy yourself?" Ares' scent cocooned her.

"We could sit on a deserted island watching coconuts grow, and I would enjoy myself as long as I'm with you."

She chuckled. "I could think of many better things to do with our time if we were alone on a deserted island."

Ares purred, and River relaxed further. Even the itchiness of her dress no longer bothered her.

Sleepiness washed over her. "I'm glad you found me, Ares."

He kissed the top of her head. "Me too, Beloved. Me too."

ARES

When they reached the estate, Ares tried to wake River, but she snored lightly at his side. He smiled and kissed her forehead, but was immediately struck by how warm her skin had become on the ride home. He felt her head with his hand and then her neck. She was several degrees hotter than she should be. Even her scent had grown stronger in the last hour. He was pretty sure he'd even be able to smell it from his room while she slept.

Panic twisted his gut, and his wolf whined.

Something. Not right.

It's fine. She just needs to rest.

Zeke opened Ares' door, and Ares gathered River in his arms and stepped from the vehicle.

Zeke looked at River and sniffed the air. "Is she okay?"

"You smell it too?"

"She smells..." Zeke cleared his throat and took a step away.

His wolf snarled. *Mine.*

Ares looked down at her flushed cheeks. "Get Lachlan and meet me outside River's room."

Zeke looked at her again and then away. "Are you sure?"

"Is there a problem?"

Zeke's jaw worked hard, and then he shook his head and hurried to the door.

Ares watched him. Something was definitely wrong.

His wolf paced, agitated.

Theo opened the front door. "Problem?"

"I hope not."

Theo sniffed the air, and his eyes widened. He looked at River and then away.

Don't. Like. Mine.

What the hell was wrong with everyone all of a sudden?

"What?" Ares demanded.

"Uh... nothing, Highness."

Ares growled and stepped into the front hallway. He looked at River. In the light, her face had grown pinker than it should be.

"Please get Princess River's mother and bring her to River's room."

Ares did not want to deal with Cherry, but things would be a hundred times worse if he didn't tell her.

Ares ascended the stairs and walked down the hallway to River's room.

She stirred in his arms. "Are we home?"

"Yes."

She scrunched up her face and scratched her neck. "I'm hot."

"I know. It's okay. I'll get you some medicine and water."

She moaned, making his wolf pace and whine.

Ares shoved open the double doors to her room, hoping he wouldn't need to call a locksmith for the second time in twenty-four hours. He strode to her bed and laid her on it. He removed his coat from her shoulders, then removed her heels and set them on the floor.

"Highness?"

Ares turned to find Lachlan in the doorway.

He kissed River's forehead. "I'll be right back."

He hurried to the doors and closed them as he stepped into the hall.

"You were there when the bullet was taken out, right?"

Lachlan looked at the closed door. "Yes."

"Who took it out?"

"Bennett."

"Did he get it all out? The whole thing?"

Lachlan's eyebrows smashed together. "I'm sure he did."

"Did he, or didn't he?"

Lachlan blinked rapidly.

"I'm sorry." Ares wrapped his arms around himself. "I'm sorry. But it's important."

Lachlan thought for a minute and then shook his head. "I thought he did. The bullet looked pretty intact."

"But it's possible he didn't?"

"It's possible."

Apollo exited his room. "What's going on?"

Ares stormed over to him, but Apollo didn't blink. Damn, he hated how Apollo could keep his cool so well. Ares had always been the one who wore his emotions on his sleeves.

"Where's Bennett?"

Apollo shrugged. "In his room."

"Get him," Ares demanded.

Apollo's eyes flashed, and he crossed his arms over his chest. "Why?"

Ares didn't want Apollo in the middle of what was happening, but there was no way he could hide it from him.

"Something's wrong with River. She has a fever, and I want to know if he missed a piece of the bullet."

Apollo's gaze flicked to River's bedroom, and he uncrossed his arms and took a step forward, but Ares pushed him in the chest.

"Is there a possibility he missed something?"

Apollo swiped Ares' hand away. "No. He's a field medic. If something is wrong with River, it's not his fault." Apollo shouldered past Ares. "Now, get the hell out of my way so I can see my mate."

Ares growled and grabbed Apollo's arm. Apollo turned and, without warning, slammed his fist into Ares' jaw. Ares let go of him just long enough for Apollo to reach River's door.

"Leave her," said Ares. "She's sleeping."

Apollo pulled out his phone and punched in a number as he opened River's doors and walked in.

Ares growled and followed him.

"Bennett. I need you. Bring your kit. It's River."

Apollo dropped his phone onto the nightstand and sat next to

River. He did what Ares had done. He touched her forehead and neck before leaning in and sniffing her. He groaned.

"She smells stronger than in the barn. What the hell is she wearing? That can't be comfortable." Apollo tried to pull her dress off. "We need to get this off her so Bennett can look at her."

"Hell no," Ares snarled. "There is no way he is going to look at my mate while she's naked."

"Well, I hate to break it to you, brother, but he's already seen her with nothing on but a sheet, so..."

"I don't care. That dress does not come off-"

"The hell it doesn't!"

All eyes went to the doorway where Cherry marched in. "Whose stupid idea was it to leave her in a frickin' straitjacket to sleep?"

Apollo cocked an eyebrow at Ares as Cherry pushed past both of them and walked to River feeling her head, then her cheek, and then her throat.

Cherry looked past the twins. "Strider."

River's tall, quiet stepfather entered the room.

"Help me get this thing off her."

Strider sat River up while Cherry unzipped the dress.

"I'd prefer if-"

"If what?" Cherry snapped. "You lot have done a bugger all good for my daughter so far. So, as far as I'm concerned, you can take your preferences and shove them right up your-"

"Cherry," Strider said softly.

She looked at him and took a deep breath before looking at Ares again.

"Until my daughter is well again, I am making the decisions. If you don't like it, I'd happily take her back to our pack doctor in the States."

She looked from Ares to Apollo.

The two shared a look, and Apollo shrugged.

Damn pussy. Couldn't even stand up to Cherry. And he was supposed to be the next king of the Lycans? Never gonna happen.

"The three of us will make decisions for her until she is better," Ares said smoothly. "You are welcome to return to the States, get your doctor, and bring him here."

"Her. Our doctor is a woman. The smarter and more logical choice, of course."

Ares ground his teeth together.

Cherry turned back to River and her dress. She pulled River's arms out one by one.

River's eyes fluttered open. "Mom? What are you doing?" She started to struggle, but Cherry grabbed her arms.

"I'm taking you out of this ridiculously tight dress. Why the hell do you let them show you off like arm candy anyway? It's so degrading."

River blinked. "I like how Ares looks at me when I wear what he wants."

Her mom threw Ares an icy glare. Ares couldn't help but smirk.

"You aren't their toy doll, River. You are you. Don't let them take it from you."

River shook her head. "You wouldn't understand. You never dressed up for Dad or Strider."

"Damn right. I like a man who takes me as I am."

A cough sounded from the door as Cherry and Strider got River's dress off her. Ares rounded on the newcomer and snarled.

Apollo jumped in front of River, shielding her from view.

"Sorry, Highnesses," said Bennett.

Ares took two steps forward. "Did you screw something up when you took that bullet out of my mate's shoulder?"

"What?" Bennett looked to Apollo.

Ares stepped forward again. "I asked you-"

Apollo stepped between the two. "That's enough. You speak to Bennett respectfully, or don't speak to him at all."

Ares' last nerve snapped. "Listen asshole-"

"No, you listen," said Apollo. "Everyone in this room cares about River. You aren't the only one. So back the fuck off so we can find out what's wrong with her."

Ares stared at Apollo, his hands clenching and unclenching at his sides. His nails lengthened, and he worked his jaw so hard he thought he might break it.

Apollo's words had Ares' wolf's hackles up, but he couldn't help but admit he was impressed by his brother's outburst. About damn time.

Ares took several deep breaths, and Theo stepped into the room.

"Ares. I know Bennett. He's a good guy. He wouldn't leave anything half-done. If Bennett says he got all of the bullet out, he got it out."

Ares looked to Theo and then back to Bennett, who hadn't flinched an inch from Ares' anger.

Ares licked his lips. "Did you get it all?"

Bennett nodded. "I did."

"Highness, why don't we step into the hall while Bennett looks at Princess River?" Theo said.

Ares looked to Apollo, then to Bennett, and back to Apollo. "He doesn't touch her. Not even for a moment."

Apollo looked like he might argue. Instead, he nodded.

Ares wanted to punch Apollo so bad his muscles twitched. Finally, he followed Theo and walked into the hall.

APOLLO

Everyone in the room let out a collectively held breath when Ares left. Apollo's wolf was crazy with worry for River, but something else as well. Something neither of them could process.

Apollo refused to let fear take over until they knew what they were dealing with.

Apollo clapped Bennett on the shoulder. "Take a look, please."

Bennett nodded and headed to the side of the bed. Strider moved to the side of the room to give Bennett access to River, but Cherry didn't move a muscle.

Bennett pulled down the sheet covering River and inspected her shoulder.

Apollo's wolf roared. *No. Touch. Mine.*

Easy. He has to touch her.

Bennett looked at it for a long minute before Cherry said, "It's not the shoulder, is it?"

Bennett shook his head. "Has she been sick before?"

Cherry shrugged. "I… I…" She looked to Strider.

"A few times," he said. "Nothing serious. A cold here and there. Once, she had the flu pretty bad. She was about fifteen."

Bennett nodded.

So not only had River's father been the one who'd cared for her, but Strider had taken over when he and Cherry got together. The dynamic in River's family was almost as strange as Apollo's.

Bennett reached into his med kit and pulled out a thermometer. Cherry turned River's head to the side, and Bennett pressed the thermometer to River's ear. A second later, it beeped loudly.

Bennett showed the thermometer to Apollo. 102.3. Shifters usually ran warm at around 100 degrees. 102 was not normal.

"She's fighting something," said Bennett. "But I don't know what."

"She complained this morning about being uncomfortable and warm," said Apollo.

"She shivered several times while we were out as well. She said she was hot but welcomed my jacket when I offered it."

Apollo turned to see Ares leaning against the wall, hands in his pockets, face a mask.

Bennett looked at her again. "Could just be the flu, maybe? Exhaustion?" He thought for a moment. "When was the last time she had her period?"

Ares growled.

"She ate her way through half the candy in the pantry today," said Apollo. "She said it was PMS. So I am assuming she will be having it sometime soon."

"Wait." Cherry's eyes widened, and she looked at Ares. "Where are her pills?"

"Her blockers? I don't think she brought them. There was no need since we'd found each other."

Cherry jumped from the bed. "You're joking. Tell me you're joking. Please."

Ares straightened. "No."

Cherry looked at River and then at Strider, Apollo, Ares, and Bennett. She grabbed her hair.

"Shit. Shit. Shit. Shit. Shit. Oh no. Please no. This is not happening. This is not." Cherry marched up to River and grabbed River's breast.

River whimpered, and her legs moved under the sheets.

Cherry looked at all of them in terror. "Get out," she whispered. "Get out. All of you. Everyone. Get out! Get out now!" The hysterical pitch in Cherry's voice made even Strider straighten.

Strider rounded the bed to where Apollo stood. "Highness, we should go."

"Hell no," said Ares. "What's going on?"

Cherry stared at him. "Get the hell out of my daughter's room, or so help me, I will kill you with my bare hands."

"Please," said Strider to Ares. "Please let Cherry be with her daughter. Whatever it is, my mate obviously has a very good reason for wanting us all to leave."

Ares looked about to argue, but then he held up a hand. "Five minutes. You get five minutes to do whatever it is you need to do, and then you will tell us what is going on, or so help me-"

"Brother, let's not finish that sentence," Apollo said.

Ares looked at him and huffed.

Apollo nodded to Strider even though his wolf snarled and barked at Apollo for leaving.

"Bennett, let's go."

Bennett collected his belongings and walked out of the room.

Apollo took one last look at River and then backed out as well. Before he closed the doors, he said, "Five minutes. Then we all want to know what is going on."

CHAPTER EIGHTEEN

CHERRY

Cherry stood inside River's bedroom and wiped the tears from her cheeks. She breathed several times, trying to calm herself and her wolf.

She'd tried. Tried so damn hard to protect her. She'd done everything she could. Everything and still… here they were. And it wasn't the worst-case scenario that Cherry had imagined; it was so much worse.

She wanted to scream. Wanted to grab River and run away with her. Wanted… what was about to happen, not to happen.

Suck it up. You screwed up. Get over it. Move on.

Cherry's wolf did nothing to soothe Cherry's fears. But then, her wolf never had. Ever since Cherry gave her heart to Strider at sixteen, her wolf had hated her. And when she'd later met River's dad, Oliver Whitetail, her fated mate, a strange, unheard-of thing had happened. Her wolf bonded with Oliver's wolf, but Cherry did not. She still longed for Strider.

For months, Cherry had fought the bond, but in the end, Strider had encouraged her to stop hurting herself and let the bond happen. Cherry had refused to leave him, and so, he'd done the honorable thing and left. Without warning. Without a goodbye. It had torn Cherry's heart out when he'd gone. And in her sorrow, her wolf had taken the initiative and forced her to mate with Oliver. And that's when Cherry had begun to hate her wolf in return. Ever since, Cherry had been torn in two. Never agreeing with her wolf and only letting her wolf out when forced to. The fated mating had almost killed Cherry, and she'd sworn never to let that happen to River.

But when River had gone into heat for the first time at the age of twelve, Cherry knew she was an Omega and had become even more determined to make sure River never went through what she had. It's why she'd started River on the blocker pills and descenting spray to begin with. She'd never expected a Lycan to show up, though. And she'd never once thought that River would be a Lycan's Omega. Let alone two.

She sucked in a deep breath, swiped at her eyes, and set her shoulder back. She needed to put on her toughest exterior now and get those two Lycan prince pups to listen to her because if they didn't… it could cost River her life.

Cherry pulled open River's bedroom doors and stepped into the hall. Both Ares and Apollo stepped up to her, their eyes expectant.

Cherry's gaze shifted to Strider, who gave her a reassuring nod.

Tell them. Tell them you failed.

Shut up!

Her wolf chuffed.

"Well," Ares demanded.

"I need to apologize," said Cherry.

"Damn right," said Ares. "You have no right to-"

"Not for that dipshit. I have to apologize for being so stupid as to think that my daughter could get through this life without me having to tell her every little thing and hold her freaking hand."

Ares and Apollo shared a look.

"What are you talking about?" asked Apollo.

Cherry looked at him. Though she didn't like either twin, Apollo at least seemed to have his crap together better than Ares. However, if Cherry had to choose one of them for River, it would have been Ares because at least she knew Ares was capable of keeping River safe.

"The pills. The ones River takes."

"The blockers?"

Cherry nodded. "They aren't normal blockers. I had them specially made for River because she's an Omega. Specially designed to… block everything."

"Yeah, she told me. She didn't even meet her wolf until Titan arrived." Ares shook his head. "I don't understand. What does that have to do with River being sick?"

Apollo's eyes widened. "Shit. You don't mean-"

"Yeah." Cherry nodded. "She's going into heat."

Ares opened his mouth, then shut it again, and turned away.

"Oh no." Strider stepped toward Cherry, but she shook her head to stop him.

She couldn't take his comfort, not now that she'd messed up so bad. If he showed her an ounce of affection, she would break down in front of her would-be sons-in-law, and that could not happen. Not if she needed to convince them of what needed to happen next.

"What happens now?" asked Apollo.

"Now, you send all of your unmated men out of the estate. I don't care how loyal they are to you. Because she isn't mated, her scent will drive all of them into a frenzy."

"That explains a lot," said Ares.

Apollo nodded. "We will have them out tonight."

Cherry nodded. "In the next hour would be best."

Ares looked at the door behind Cherry. "What about River? What do we do for her?"

"You? Well, you and your brother will be taking those big dicks you keep swinging around and put them to use easing her heat."

Ares spun around, and both brothers blinked.

"I'm sorry," said Apollo. "Did you say both of us?"

"I did."

"Hell no," said Ares. "There is no way-"

"Look," said Cherry. "I tended to our Luna when she went into heat once. Our Alpha was gone on pack business when it happened. I thought she'd die from the way her temperature rose. She clawed at her skin until she drew blood because the pain was so bad, and trust me, we bought her every toy we could find. Nothing worked. Nothing but sex with her mate. And even then, that took a couple days to pass with him servicing her. And she was mated already. I have no idea what will happen to River because she isn't mated yet. All I know is that the two of you are going to have to suck it up and take care of her until this passes."

"No," said Ares. "No way am I going to let him touch her, let alone get in bed with my mate."

"You think I want your manicured nails and two-thousand-dollar suited ass anywhere near *my* mate?" Apollo retorted. "I'd rather die fighting you for her than know you'd touched one silken strand of her hair."

Ares took a step toward Apollo and growled. Apollo rose to the challenge, and his eyes went black.

"Stop it," Cherry yelled. "Believe me when I say I know how it feels to share the one you love with someone else. It's hard. Harder than anything else you will ever do in your life. But if you care for her, if you love her, you will put that aside and do this. For her. It's the only way."

Cherry looked between the brothers and, for a moment, was afraid she would have to physically stop them from killing one another. Tension crackled in the air, and no one moved. Finally, Ares spoke.

"There is no way in hell I'm getting into bed with him."

Cherry fought back an audible sigh. "Don't be stupid. River would never want that. You'll have to take turns."

"And how do we decide who goes first?" Apollo's eyes turned back to their natural color.

Cherry looked at him. "You'll go first."

"I found her first. She chose me first," said Ares.

"Unclench for a minute and let me finish," Cherry shot back. "Apollo will need to be with her first because he is the oldest and first in line for the throne. It only makes sense."

Ares went to protest, but she held up her hand to stop him.

"Do you ever shut that giant trap of yours?" She continued. "Second, because Apollo will be gentler with her. She's gonna need that in the beginning. But after the first twenty-four hours, she won't want gentle anymore. She's going to… want more. Need more. And I get the feeling you will be the one to help with that, Ares."

Again, silence stretched out for a long, tense minute as her words sank in.

"Is there anything else we should know?" Ares tore his gaze from Apollo to look at her.

"I'm pretty sure both of you know how this works. I don't have to draw diagrams or anything, do I?"

"No," they both said.

"So are you suggesting that I just sit in my room, smelling River and hearing her have sex with Apollo for twenty-four hours?" Ares asked.

Cherry shrugged. "If you're into that kind of thing, go for it. Personally, I would get a hotel and wait until we call you."

Ares shook his head. "I don't like it. What if it goes wrong?"

"What, you think I don't know how to make love to River?" Apollo snorted. "You may think me an idiot, but I promise you I will give River everything she needs."

"If you could do that, she wouldn't need me to come in and finish her off, would she?"

Apollo growled.

"Knock it off," Cherry yelled. "You two either want to help her, or you don't. This macho I-hate-my-brother bullshit needs to stop. If it doesn't and you two can't figure this out, River will pay. So are you two gonna Lycan up and do what you are meant to do, or are you going to pussy out and make her suffer?"

The two brothers stared at each other without speaking for several seconds.

"Just because you get to have her first doesn't mean she's yours," said Ares. "The only reason I'm even considering this is because it's what she needs."

"And the only reason I'm even considering letting you lay a finger on her is because I love her more than I hate you," Apollo responded.

"Good," said Cherry. "Then it's settled. Now, you two get the other males out of here and close all the doors and windows. We need to contain her scent as much as possible. You never know who could smell it and come knocking, and we don't need rogues rushing this estate with your guards gone. And get some rest. You're both gonna need it." Cherry turned to leave but stopped. "Lastly, don't even think about going into her room because I'll be back in ten minutes with a blanket and pillow camped out on the other side of that bedroom door. And I will not hesitate to stab anyone who tries to come in uninvited. She needs to sleep, too. Got it?"

Without waiting for a reply, Cherry walked toward Strider, who lifted himself off the wall and followed her down the hallway to a back staircase, where she ascended to an upper floor. She walked to the third door and shoved it open before doubling over and letting the tears flow.

The door closed quietly behind her, and then Strider's warm hand pressed into her back. Cherry let out all of the tears she'd held back and then ran to the bed and grabbed a giant pillow. Plunging her face into it, she screamed as hard as she could. She screamed a second time and then a third before stopping and sitting on the edge of the bed.

Weak. Unfit.

How could she have been so stupid? How could she not have anticipated something like this happening? Why didn't she have a contingency plan?

Because River wasn't supposed to be a Lycan king's mate, that's why. Because she was supposed to just take her pills and stay under the radar. How was Cherry to know the pills wouldn't work on Alpha Lycans?

A minute passed, and Strider sat beside her and took the pillow from her face.

He pulled her into his strong arms, and her wolf grumbled.

"It's not your fault," Strider soothed.

"Isn't it?"

"You can't fight nature. She is what she is, just as you are what you are. You staved it off as long as you could, but this was always going to happen at some point. The pills couldn't last forever. Or she would forget to take them. Or run out. She had to go into heat sometime."

"I should have told her the truth. I should have told her what the pills did. Then maybe-"

"It's too late for that, Love. You did what you thought best."

"But I was wrong."

Strider lifted her chin to look into his soft, gray eyes.

"You can't be right all the time." He kissed her.

A flutter raced through Cherry's belly like it always did when Strider kissed her. The way it had since she was sixteen years old, skinny dipping with him at the lake under the moonlight. He still had the same beautiful, soft brown eyes and shaggy hair now tinged with streaks of gray, but she didn't care. He was the only one who understood what she'd been through because he'd been through it, too. The only one who loved her despite her faults. The only one who knew the real her- not the mother, not the enforcer, but the woman she wished she'd become.

He was hers, and she was his. Always had been, always would be.

He went to break the kiss, but she pulled his lips back to hers. She needed him.

Her wolf snarled.

Shut it, bitch. You had your mate. This one is mine.

Cherry broke the kiss and pushed Strider back on the bed. She pulled off his classic rock band t-shirt. The sight of his lean, muscular body never stopped being her favorite sight.

Cherry smiled. *Her love. Her wolf. Her mate.*

He always knew just what she needed.

CHAPTER NINETEEN

RIVER

River awoke feeling prickly all over. She groaned as the sheets felt like gravel on her skin.

She opened her eyes to darkness. She looked around for a light but had no idea where one was. She scanned for her phone, trying to remember where she'd put it. She didn't even remember getting back to the estate the night before. What was going on?

She sat up, and the room spun; the air felt like a blanket suffocating her. She peered at the wall, where she remembered a window had been, and got to her feet, wobbling. Instantly, she knew she was naked because she could feel every inch of her lady parts rubbing against her legs. What the hell?

She went to touch herself and found her body swollen and hot. That couldn't be good. She tried to remember what she'd been taught in biology class about when your privates were cold, it meant you were close to freezing to death. If they were hot and swollen, did that mean she was close to overheating? Something told her that wasn't the case. Either way, she moved disjointedly to the curtains and pushed them aside before grabbing the window and cranking it open. The fresh air washed over her bare skin, making it pebble and offering a slight relief.

River moaned in satisfaction. She breathed in deep and was struck by a scent.

"What the hell?"

River turned to find Cherry lying on the floor by the doors. Cherry wiped the sleep from her eyes, looked at River, and then noticed the open window.

Cherry leapt to her feet and raced for the window, cranking it shut again.

"Mom?" River stared at Cherry.

Cherry pushed River back from the window and closed the curtains again. "Don't open that."

"It's stifling in here."

Her mom didn't answer. Instead, she sniffed River and then looked her up and down. River pulled the top sheet closer around herself.

"Mom, what are you doing in here?"

Cherry didn't speak. Instead, she blew out a breath and stretched her muscles, rubbing her neck.

River watched for a moment, and then her patience snapped.

"Mom! What are you doing in here?"

Cherry groaned. "Stop yelling. I'm exhausted."

"Why are you sleeping on my floor?"

"To keep your two mates out of here." Cherry walked over and sat on River's bed before groaning.

"Why can't I open the window?" The sheet slipped off River's torso, and she looked down. "Why am I naked?"

"Because I figured you would be more comfortable that way." Cherry didn't look at her.

"What?" River scratched at her arms, which felt hot and prickly once again. She licked her lips. "I need something to drink."

Cherry nodded.

"Are you gonna tell me what is going on?"

Cherry stopped. "Do you want water or to know what is going on?"

"Both."

"Well, pick the order. I can't get you water and tell you what's going on at the same time."

River growled. Her wolf's tail swished in agitation. She paced and panted, acting… weird, which made River all the twitchier.

"Tell me first, then water."

Cherry looked at her for a moment and then nodded. "Okay, the short version is, you are going into heat, and your mates need to help you through it, or it will be excruciating and could end up killing you."

River blinked twice. "I'm sorry, what?"

Cherry blew out a breath. "The pills I gave you that you've taken since you were twelve?"

"Yeah."

"You stopped taking them."

"When I found Ares, I didn't need to hide anymore."

"They weren't just so others couldn't smell you. They also kept you from going into full heat. But you stopped taking them after you met Ares, which means you had nothing blocking you from going into a full-blown heat like when you were twelve. And now you've found your mates, and I guess taking the blockers for so long and stopping sent your wolf and moon cycle into overdrive, and, well, here we are."

River tried to process her mom's words. She was going into heat? Like the first time?

"But… I'm not mated," said River weakly. "Can't you just get me whatever you gave me that first time?"

"It's too late. I won't get here in time. And you not being mated compounds matters, but they've both agreed to take turns helping you through the next few days."

River's eyebrows smashed together. "They? Apollo and Ares agreed to help me, how?"

Cherry huffed and rolled her eyes. "How do you think, River? They're gonna do what they've wanted to do since the moment they met you. And you will want them just as bad, if not more. You are going to want and need them to have sex with you. A lot of sex. And you will need them to knot you as well. It will be the only thing short of knocking you unconscious that will ease the need starting inside you."

Sex. She needed to have sex with Ares and Apollo? Both of them? A lot? Part of her cheered to get what she wanted from both of them. But the other part…

"They agreed to this?"

"They don't have a choice if they don't want to hear you crying in agony for the next several days."

"Did you say this could kill me?"

Cherry shrugged. "Technically, yes. It hasn't happened in a long time, but it is possible if you don't get what you need, your temperature could keep rising, and you could die."

River pulled her knees to her chest and wrapped her arms

around them. An itch started between her legs, and she fought the urge to rub it.

She took in all of Cherry's words and let them play and replay in her mind until she couldn't take any more and blew out a breath.

Cherry handed River the glass. She gulped it and then handed it back. River hadn't even noticed Cherry leaving to get it.

"Okay. I am assuming this isn't going to be a threesome type of thing. That not only would be weird, but they would most likely kill each other, and that would defeat the point."

"Apollo will take the first shift."

That surprised River. She couldn't believe Ares would ever have agreed to that.

"He's the oldest, and he will be gentler with you. You'll want Ares in the end, though, and I'm sure he will be able to satisfy you more aggressively."

River's cheeks heated. "Thanks for that, but TMI, Mom. TMI."

Cherry shrugged. "I figured you should know what was coming over the next few days."

"I should have known what was coming for the last decade."

Cherry licked her lips. "I thought what I did was best. I can't explain why. I just did. But I was wrong. I'm sorry."

River had to consciously keep her mouth from falling open. Her mom both apologized and said she was wrong. In the same sentence. Two things she couldn't remember her mom ever saying. River watched Cherry for a minute, and for the first time, she saw pain and fear in her mom's eyes.

"You did the best you could."

Cherry opened her mouth, but then closed it again.

River rubbed her arms. "Well, I already feel hot and sticky, and my lady parts are swollen, and I could use a cool shower."

Cherry nodded. "You shower, and I'll get you some food. You'll need your strength."

Cherry turned to leave.

"Mom?"

Cherry turned back.

"Thank you for all you've done for me. I know this is uncomfortable, but I'm glad you're here." River's throat clenched, and she tried to swallow down a lump.

Cherry gave her a sad smile. "Me too, baby girl."

River's chest squeezed. She couldn't remember the last time her mom called her that.

River's wolf panted and whined. She'd barely become conscious when an aching, thrumming need pulsed through her. She grumbled and then whimpered. Her skin felt prickly and warm, but she no longer felt agitated. Now she felt… horny. She'd never wanted sex so much in her life.

So this was happening. She was going into heat. Full-blown, all-out heat. She shook her head. This was not how she had hoped things would go for her and her mates.

A soft knock sounded on her door. She pushed at her hair, which she'd not even brushed after her shower, before gobbling down everything Cherry brought her to eat and falling asleep.

No one would want to have sex with her, looking like a big foot in a thunderstorm. At least she didn't stink.

"Come in," she called.

The doors opened, and Apollo entered. His scent overpowered her, making her need ratchet up even higher. She held back an audible moan.

"Hey, Kitten. How are you feeling?"

Was he serious? A wave of need shot through her, and she whined.

Apollo moved to her side in an instant. He reached up and touched her face. The feel of his skin on hers made her moan louder.

She stared at him, and he watched her, unsure. Did he not want her anymore?

"How did you know I was awake?"

"I heard you."

"Were you right outside my door?"

He shook his head. "Ever since you... started... my senses and wolf have become more acutely attuned to you. I heard your breathing from my room and could tell when you woke up."

Damn. She thought about making a joke, but the strange look on his face and the rigidity of his body made her stop.

She swallowed hard. "I understand if you don't want to do this. I'm sorry you've been put in this position."

His eyebrows drew together. "Why are you sorry? You're the one taking the brunt of what is happening."

"Because I know this isn't what you wanted."

He chuckled. "Are you kidding me? I've wanted to make love to you since I smelled you in the hallway that first day."

"Yes, but-"

He pressed his finger to her lips and then cupped her cheek. "I know that this isn't how either of us saw our first time being together going, but what does it matter how we got here? We're here."

"You don't look like you want to be."

"Honestly?"

"Of course." Though unsure, she wanted to hear what would come next.

"I'm trying to be a gentleman. Every inch of me and my wolf wants to take you right now, and just holding back is a test of restraint I never thought I would have to face."

River smiled and turned her face to kiss his palm before opening her mouth and sucking his finger into it. Apollo's eyes closed, and he shuddered.

She swirled his finger in her mouth, tasting and feeling it with her tongue. A moment passed, and Apollo ripped his finger away and replaced it with his lips. River grabbed onto him and pulled him closer. She needed his touch, his taste, him.

She kissed him harder, claiming his mouth. Apollo threaded his hands into her hair and tugged lightly, making her mewl. He broke the kiss and peppered his way down the side of her throat.

"Apollo," she choked out.

A growl escaped him as he licked over her collarbone and down to the top of where the sheet covered her.

"Apollo, wait." She couldn't believe the words came out of her mouth.

He stopped. "Are you all right? Do you not want this? Do you not want me?"

The fear in his eyes shot straight through her.

She shook her head. "No. I mean, yes, I want you. I just… I have to know that you are okay with me also needing Ares. I know I should have chosen between you sooner, and I'm sorry for the pain this is putting you through, but-"

Apollo kissed her. "I understand you didn't ask for this, just like we didn't. I don't want to think of Ares. I just want to be here with you. This is our time, and when it's over, I'll go and think only about the memories of you in my arms."

River's bottom lip quivered. "I don't deserve you."

He brushed her cheek with his knuckles. "Kitten, you deserve so much more than I alone can give you. I'm starting to understand that."

What did that mean? Did that mean he was okay with her not choosing between them?

She didn't get a chance to ask because Apollo slid his arms under her and pulled her and the sheet to him. She wrapped her arms around his neck.

"Are we going somewhere?"

He nodded. "To my room."

She realized for the first time that she hadn't been in his or Ares' rooms. A thrill of anticipation whirled through her to know that he took her somewhere so private and intimate. His place.

He carried her across the hall and opened the door. His scent overpowered her. She looked around, not surprised to see his décor consisted of beautiful yet simple furniture. A large wooden bed that reminded her of the bed she'd slept in at the cabin. A large entertainment center occupied one wall, filled with the finest electronics available. The room rounded out with an electric fireplace, a heavy desk, and a dresser. An ancient-looking rug covered the wooden floors, and an old quilt covered the king-sized bed with jersey sheets.

He laid her on the bed, and the soft sheets caressed her skin. River watched as Apollo unbuttoned his shirt, revealing his muscular physique. A ripple of desire tore through her as he unbuckled his belt and slid off his jeans. She took in his hard-muscled body.

Every glorious inch of him was followed by an even more beautiful line, muscle, or sinew. Another wave of need washed through her, and she stood and let the sheet drop from her body.

A mixture of desire and nervousness battled within her as she stood, waiting to see his reaction.

Apollo stepped up to her and kissed her tenderly. "You are so beautiful, River."

His words shot straight through her, and her wolf howled.

"Apollo, I need you," she whispered. "Make love to me."

He kissed her again, and this time, his mouth heated with need. He wrapped his arms around her and guided her back to his bed, where he laid her down and then kissed the length of her body.

River fisted her hands in the sheets. Her need growing with each passing moment.

"Apollo." She could barely get the word out from all the emotions and sensations running through her. Her wolf got down on all fours, butt in the air, ready for Apollo to take them. Her body hummed with the need to feel him inside her, and her mind could only pray Ares wasn't anywhere that he could hear or smell them.

Apollo bit the inside of her thigh, and she gasped.

"Apollo, stop teasing."

He bit her hip. "I'm not. I'm trying to make this last longer for you."

She grabbed his hair. "Trust me, there will be enough opportunities to draw things out later. Right now, I need you inside me."

His eyes turned black, and he prowled up her body, settling between her spread legs. He kissed her, and she lapped at his tongue greedily. A painful wave of need rushed through her, but dissolved the moment he entered her.

River clawed at his back and moaned at the feel of him. So big.

So hard. So amazing. He filled her so entirely that pain mixed with pleasure, and she couldn't concentrate on anything except him.

Apollo's arms shook as he kissed her. He stopped and leaned his forehead to hers. He breathed in and out harshly. His fangs descended and then retracted.

She touched his face, making him open his eyes to look at her. "Are you okay?"

He shook his head. "My wolf... he's trying to take over... he wants..."

"What? Tell me what he wants. What you want."

"I want to bite you. To mark you and make you mine."

River's wolf wanted the same thing.

"Then bite me, Apollo. Bite me and make me yours."

He looked at her uncertainly. "Are you sure? If I do this..."

She kissed him hard and bit his lower lip, drawing blood.

Apollo growled and then broke his lips away. His fangs lengthened once more. River turned her head to the side, and he thrust into her again. She clung to him as more sensations raced through her, hot as fire but sharp as an ice shard.

He rocked into her a third time, and that was all it took to get her on the edge.

"Apollo now," she commanded.

He obeyed her plea, and he lowered his fangs to her neck. He bit her hard enough to break the skin, and she cried out as he rocked into her again, making her explode. Her wolf overtook her, and River's fang descended, and she bit into Apollo's muscular neck, his blood bursting into her mouth, and her wolf howled.

River wrapped her legs around his waist as her body shattered around him, and he rocked into her again and again until his fang disengaged, and he roared. Every muscle in his body tensed as he continued to rock into her several more times.

He kissed her long and languidly, making her mewl with delight. Purring erupted from Apollo's chest and washed over her, making her relax and kiss him harder.

After several minutes, Apollo pulled away and looked deep into her eyes.

"I love you, River. I need you to know that. To know that no matter what happens in the future, I am yours, and you are mine, no matter what."

A touch of sadness crossed his features, and she cupped his cheek.

"Don't say it back. I don't want you to say it. Not now. I want you to say it when you are ready, but I needed you to know."

River went to unwrap her legs, but he stopped her.

"I wouldn't do that if I were you, Kitten. That would be quite painful for both of us."

She tried to understand his words and then realized what he meant. They were knotted.

She wrapped her legs back around him, and he dropped down on top of her and kissed her again. Bliss washed over her, leaving her both happy and sated.

He loved her. He'd said he loved her. And they'd marked each other. She'd chosen him. Her thoughts traveled to Ares. What would he say? What would he do? A pang of guilt swept through her as minutes later, Apollo slid out of her and pulled her into his chest. She swirled her fingers in the soft smattering of hair that sprouted there. She nipped and kissed his skin, and as she did, desire flooded her again.

She groaned.

"What's wrong?" He pulled her into his arms.

"It's… not over."

He chuckled. "Good, because that is not the impression I want to leave you with for our first night together."

Apollo rolled her onto her back as another, more forceful wave pushed through her core.

He suckled one breast while palming the other. "Don't worry, Kitten. I know just what you need."

CHAPTER TWENTY

APOLLO

More than twenty-four hours later, both Apollo and his wolf had never known the meaning of the word exhaustion like they did in that moment. He could barely lift his arms or sit up. He worked out, but… this was like a ten-hour plank session. He had no idea how many times he and River made love. No idea how he'd managed to get there or get her there so many times. And no idea how neither of them hadn't dehydrated and died. They'd made love in the bed, on the floor, on his desk, in the bath, by the fire, against the wall, and pretty much on every other solid surface in his room. And a few not-so-solid surfaces that had almost broken. He'd never made love in so many different ways in his life. He was reasonably certain that even the Kama Sutra didn't include a few of those positions in the books.

She'd only been asleep for twenty minutes when a moan escaped her, and his erection twitched. The pain that shot through him made him wince. It surprised him that either of them still had skin left to hurt.

He traced a finger down her arm, and she wiggled closer to him and wrapped her leg over his. Her soft breasts smashed against his chest, and he placed a hand at the small of her back. She was so beautiful. Even with her skin flushed a brighter pink color due to her high temperature, she was still the most beautiful creature he'd ever seen. And she was his.

He wasn't sure if it had been the third or fourth time he'd made love to her when his wolf had finally backed off, satisfied with their mating bond. Even as he lay there, Apollo could feel the white ribbon that now permanently connected him to his mate.

His mate. His Omega. His High Luna. His. Apollo couldn't get the word out of his head. His. He'd never dreamed that having a fated mate could make him feel so… complete.

River whined again and rolled over.

His tongue clung to the roof of his mouth. He needed water.

Apollo slid to the edge of the bed and stood. The ceiling and the floor traded places, and he closed his eyes and leaned on the night-stand for support to keep from toppling over.

Not good. The world spun behind his eyelids, and he fought to stay on his feet. After several moments, he swallowed hard and went to the bathroom. Turning on the cold water, he stuck his head under the faucet and let the shock of the spray bring him to his senses. He gulped down several huge mouthfuls, scrubbed his face, and ran his hands through his hair.

Water dripped down his torso, and his muscles shook with fatigue. He tried to stretch his arms, but it only made things worse. He took several more big gulps of water and then sucked in a deep breath.

He wondered how often females went into heat. As much as he loved making love to River, he was pretty sure it would take him at least six months to fully recover from just one night of her being in heat.

River moaned in the bedroom and called his name.

The sound shot straight through him, making his wolf jump to his feet, ready to keep going.

Sorry, bud, said Apollo. *The heart is willing, but the body is weak.*

His wolf growled as both of them knew what came next.

Trust me. I don't want him near her, but this isn't about us. It's about her. She needs him just as much as she needed us. We have to do this for her.

His wolf snarled and then whined. Apollo felt the same.

He walked shakily back into his room and grabbed a pair of lounge pants from his dresser. Pulling them on without falling over-took more effort than it should have.

"Apollo," River murmured, pulling her face from the pillow.

Apollo sat next to her on the bed. Her skin radiated heat far greater than when they'd started.

Her eyes fluttered open, glassy and unfocused.

She looked over him and then frowned. "You're leaving me, aren't you?"

Her words punched him in the gut.

He swallowed hard. "You don't need me now, Kitten. You need him."

River reached for Apollo and pulled his hand to her mouth. She kissed his knuckles before rubbing them on her cheek.

"Maybe... maybe we just need to keep going a bit more," she offered. "Just a few more times, and maybe it will stop."

He chuckled. "I don't think I have a few more times in me. I am more than happy to stay here and give you everything you desire with every other part of my body, but we both know that it wouldn't help."

"But we're mated now."

Apollo couldn't believe the words about to leave his mouth. He willed himself not to speak them, even though they were true.

"It's not enough," he finally said. "I'm not enough."

She stared at him and touched his cheek. "Don't say that. I love you, Apollo. You're my mate. You will always be enough."

Apollo's chest squeezed so tight he couldn't get words out. She loved him. He knew she did. But for some reason, it didn't matter. The Moon Goddess decided that River's fate wasn't tied to him alone but to Ares as well. He'd tried so hard to deny it. Tried so hard to make it not true. But it didn't matter. In the end, she belonged to both of them. And no matter how many more hours he spent trying to relieve her need, until she had Ares, it wouldn't stop.

"I'll be back," he said.

"Where are you going?"

"To get you something to drink." He stood, leaned over her, and kissed her head as his wolf tugged on his restraints, trying to get free and force Apollo to stay with her.

"Can I have a soda?" Her eyelids fluttered closed again.

"Of course." Apollo kissed her once more, but she was already asleep.

He picked up his shirt and phone from the floor and then went to the bedroom door.

“Apollo?”

“Yes, Kitten.”

“I need you to know, really know. I’m glad you were with me first. That we bonded first. Even though we met second, doesn’t put you in second place in my heart. You have every ounce of love in my body. You are my mate. My Alpha. And I am your Omega. No matter what else happens. I am yours. Always and forever."

He looked at her for only a moment before slipping into the hallway, so she could see the pain he couldn't conceal in his eyes.

Every step he took from where she lay made his wolf go into even more of a frenzy.

We have to, he said repeatedly. *She needs him.*

His wolf didn't buy it.

Apollo wasn't surprised to see Cherry and Strider sitting at the kitchen table, drinking a large bottle of whiskey. They looked up as he entered. He made his way to the fridge and opened it. Grabbing a bottle of freshly squeezed OJ, he chugged it, set the bottle on the counter, and wiped his mouth.

He splayed his palms on the granite surface and stared at it, surrounded by the feel, the touch, and the taste of his mate. His mate. River was his mate. But not only his.

"Well?" Cherry asked.

Apollo looked at her to find the bags beneath her eyes, deep as bruises.

"Call him."

Cherry nodded and pulled out her phone.

Apollo didn't listen as Cherry told Ares to get to the house. He went to the pantry, grabbed a six-pack of cola, and a bucket. He filled the bucket with ice and then set all the items, along with a glass, onto the tray.

He took a breath, pulled out his phone, and texted Bennett.

Pick up at the kitchen door.

His phone beeped almost immediately.

I'll be there in five.

He shoved his phone back in his pocket. "She's thirsty. She'll need the sugar. She's hotter than yesterday, so the ice will help, too."

He couldn't meet Cherry's eye, so he walked toward the back door.

"Is she... okay?"

Apollo nodded. "She's fine. I just..."

"What?"

"I don't understand. We bonded. She bit me, and I bit her, but still, I could tell she needed something else... someone else. She really does belong to both of us, doesn't she?"

When Cherry didn't answer, he stepped toward the door, but Cherry's words stopped him.

"Are you okay?"

Her face held none of the tough vibrato he'd always seen from her. Only the worry of a mother who loved her daughter.

"I'm fine," he lied before turning again.

"I'm sorry, Apollo. I'm sorry that this is happening to you and River."

He snorted. "Not Ares?"

She shrugged. "That cocky bastard can deal with it."

Apollo chuckled, and so did Cherry.

"Thanks, Cherry. Call me when the coast is clear to come back."

She nodded.

"Oh, and you probably want to move her out of my room before Ares arrives. I'm pretty sure that won't end well."

"Apollo? Thank you."

Apollo wondered how much Cherry had had to drink because, according to River, 'I'm sorry' and 'thank you' were not part of Cherry's vocabulary.

He threw her a weak smile. "The pleasure was all mine."

He walked out the door into the chilly evening air without another word. His bare feet soaked in the cool cement, sending a chill through him. He breathed deeply and then sat on the steps, waiting for Bennett.

He hung his head in his hands, and a tear dropped between his feet.

CHAPTER TWENTY-ONE

ARES

Ares rushed up the front steps of the estate and threw the front door wide. He dropped his coat to the floor and shrugged off his suit jacket. Loosening his tie, he took the stairs three at a time. He'd been in the middle of a Zoom meeting when his phone rang with Cherry's number. Without saying goodbye, he shut his laptop and raced to the waiting car.

The last thirty hours had been the hardest of his life. About halfway through, he'd feared that perhaps Apollo and River had mated and that there would be no more need for him, but he'd refused to give in to fear. He knew River was his. Knew they were meant for each other. Even so, the thoughts of Apollo being with her had consumed him until the call. And now, as he rushed toward her bedroom, all he could think of was seeing her. Being able to look at her and know she was okay.

Even before Ares opened her doors, her scent shot straight

through him and made him hard as the North Pole in the middle of winter.

His heart beat wildly as he took in the room. Cherry held a wet rag to River's head. Half a dozen empty cola cans lay strewn over the bed and floor.

Cherry looked at him and scowled. "Took your time getting here. Did you take the scenic route?"

Ares growled. "I got here as fast as the car would go."

Cherry scoffed. "Then you should have run. Can't you see the pain she's in?"

Ares stepped forward, and Strider appeared from a dark corner of the room and walked to Cherry.

"Come on, Love. You've done all you can." Strider kissed Cherry's head and pulled her hands from River's face.

Cherry grabbed him, and Ares swore he could smell panic on her. He took her in, noticing she wore the same clothes from two days prior, and her hair looked like she hadn't brushed it in a month. Even her eyes seemed puffy and sunken in.

As Strider led Cherry out of the room, it struck Ares. No matter how she appeared or acted, Cherry truly loved River.

His chest squeezed, remembering his own mother.

"Cherry?" he said softly.

She turned to him.

"I'll take care of her. I promise on my life. I'm going to take care of her, whatever she needs."

An expression of respect came over Cherry's face, and then she nodded. "You'd better, or I'll eat your balls for breakfast."

The door closed behind them, and Ares couldn't help but smile.

River moaned and rolled over. He undid the French cuffs on his shirt and then threw off his tie, unbuttoning his crisp shirt as he sat on the bed and touched her too-bright cheek.

Her eyes fluttered open, and she tried to focus on him. "Ares?"

"Yes, Beloved. I'm here."

She whimpered, and he'd barely stripped off his shirt before she crawled into his lap naked and needy. Her lips clamped down on his, and his wolf howled. He tangled his hands in her hair, and she kissed him frantically, her hot hands roaming his skin.

She kissed down his neck, and his arousal strained, almost bursting the zipper.

She ran her hands down the front of his pants and rubbed him through them.

Ares growled as she licked up his throat and kissed him again. Her fingers fumbled with his belt buckle, and she grumbled in frustration.

Her scent invaded him, making him want her all the more, but then a second scent hit him. *Apollo.*

Ares wolf snarled. *Ours. Our mate.*

Ares broke the kiss. "River."

Her mouth slammed down on his again. He groaned as one hand rubbed him through his pants, and the other tried to undo his belt again.

Ours. Mine. Mate. Claim.

Ares fought between wanting her and needing to wash Apollo away. It took every ounce of strength he had, but he grabbed her wrists and pulled his mouth from hers.

She looked at him, bewildered through bleary eyes.

"River, stop."

"You… don't want me? Is it because of Apollo? Did it break us?"

Ares wolf roared in pain, and Ares took a deep breath to keep from finding his twin and ripping his throat out. But in the moment that he fought to calm himself, he realized that nothing had changed for him. His wolf still wanted her. He still wanted her. And they both still knew she was meant for them.

He opened his eyes and looked at her.

"Do you still feel like I'm meant to be your mate?"

River nodded vigorously. "I need you, Ares. I want you."

"Then that's all that matters."

"But-"

"That's all I care about. My wolf is still telling me you are his. And I know in my heart you are still mine. I don't care what happened with Apollo. I only care what happens between us. Here. Now. But I need something from you first."

"Anything."

"I need to get his scent off you."

She nodded. "Shower?"

He purred. "Absolutely."

Ares stood with her still wrapped around his waist and covered her with a sheet before opening the door and walking down to his room with her. He forced himself not to look at Apollo's door as they passed, but he couldn't help it as his gaze flicked that direction, wondering if Apollo was in there.

Damn, he hoped so. He wanted Apollo to hear and smell every last thing he would do with River.

River pulled his chin back to her, and she kissed him. He kissed her hard and stopped at his door long enough to press her into it and kiss down her neck and over her breasts.

"Ares. I need you."

"And I you."

A spasm ripped through her, and she cried out, clawing at his back.

"Ares, make it stop."

His wolf whimpered at the pain in her voice.

He kissed her again and opened his bedroom door. "Don't worry. I'm going to give you exactly what you need."

He didn't bother turning on the light or stripping off his pants. He slid out of his dress shoes and headed straight for the shower. The lights turned on automatically, illuminating the black slate enclosure with a river rock floor and a giant overhead rain shower.

Towels and several lotions and oils lay on the cream travertine counter, just as he'd instructed.

He stepped into the shower, pressed her against the cool tile, and reached for the water, turning it on. Frigid ice shards pelted his back as he shielded her from the icy blast. She clung to him until the water warmed, then he turned and let it wash over her.

She sighed as the water hit her skin. He held her up, letting the water soak her body. She smiled and relaxed before her face contorted in pain, and her nails dug into his arms.

Ares swooped in and kissed her as he trailed his fingers down her body to the apex between her legs.

She moaned into his mouth as he traced her hot and swollen sensitive parts. As he slid his fingers inside her, she bucked her hips toward him.

"More," she panted. "I need more."

She didn't even bother trying to undo his belt again. Instead, she sliced through it with a long, sharp claw and then ripped open the zipper of his pants.

Ares growled at her strength and feistiness. His manhood jutted outward as she shoved his pants and underwear down around his hips.

"Ares. Please. You promised that if I asked you, you'd make love to me. You promised at my show."

He kissed her again, swirling his tongue with hers. He had promised her. It wasn't how he'd seen their first time going, but that didn't matter. His mate was begging him for help, and by the goddess, he wouldn't deny her.

With a gentle thrust, Ares eased himself inside her. Instantly, his vision darkened, and his fangs descended as his wolf howled in ecstasy. Her warmth surrounded him, and he almost came right there. He forced himself to stop. This was for her. Her needs, not his.

He waited, kissing her under the warm spray until she wriggled in his grip. She dug her heels into his rear and pushed herself up before sliding down on him again.

Ares growled when she did it a second time and then a third before her muscles clenched around him, and her head fell back against the wall.

She cried out his name, and he rocked into her with hard, long thrusts. She hadn't even finished her climax when he rolled up his legs and coursed across his hips and back.

Ares roared her name as he came hard and fast. Every instinct inside him told him to bite her, to make her his, but he fought back and tried to focus on just her being with him.

Her climax passed, and she sagged in his arms. Eyes hooded, she smiled and touched his cheek.

He leaned in and kissed her softly before trailing his lips down to her breasts and kissing and sucking on them until she made little whimpering sounds.

A surge rippled through her, and she panted again.

"Ares..."

"Tell me what you need, River."

"I need you. Hard and fast. But I don't understand. Don't you want to give me your knot?"

Ares' stomach quivered. Of course, he did. Hell, he wanted to give it to her every time they made love, but he wasn't sure if that was what she wanted.

"Is that what you want?"

She reached between their bodies and stroked him. "I need you. I need your knot. I need all of you."

"Absolutely. But not in here. Let me wash you first."

Ares set her on her feet, and she wobbled uncertainly. He kept a tight grip on one of her hips as he pulled a bar of soap from the soap dish and slid it down her body. She shivered and turned her head, exposing her neck to him. So she had mated with Apollo.

His jaw clenched, and his wolf whined.

Ares swallowed hard, seeing the mark from Apollo and the old scar from Titan.

Third, to the party is third best, he heard Titan laugh.

Anger bubbled to the surface, but he pushed it away. No. He wouldn't let either of them ruin this for him or River because neither of them mattered. In the end, what she'd needed was him. Not them, him. She'd called his name and needed his knot to complete her, and there was nothing they could do about it.

Ares washed her, turned off the water, and stepped out of his ruined suit pants to grab a lush white towel. He wrapped it around her and carried her to his bed. He took in her beautiful, naked curves for the first time. He trailed his palms down the curve of her breast to the small of her waist and back over the curve of her hip.

"Goddess above you are perfect." He pinched her nipple, and she arched off the bed and gasped. "I want to touch and taste every molecule of you."

"Yes," she breathed. "But first." She wrapped her legs around his waist and flipped him onto his back.

Damn.

She straddled his hips and pressed her palms into his chest. "I need something else."

Ares had never been so turned on in his life. Not even when they'd been on the dance floor, and he'd seen her in that bustier and miniskirt.

"Use me and take what you need."

She didn't have to be asked twice. She positioned herself over him, and instead of gently sliding down on him, she impaled herself on his shaft and cried out.

Ares was about to ask her if she was okay when she did it again. The sensation of being exposed to the cool air of the room and then the sudden heat of her body made Ares strain not to climax. Goddess above, she felt good.

Again, she speared herself onto him and cried out. Ares looked down to see a rivulet of blood trickle over his hip.

"River stop. You're hurting yourself."

"I need more," she panted. "Harder. I need it harder. I need you to give it to me like you promised, Ares."

"I've been trying to be gentle, Little Wolf. You're so small and soft."

River growled in frustration and raked her nails down his chest, opening his skin.

Ares hissed, and she leaned in and licked the lines of blood from his torso just as they began to seal shut.

When she finished, she bent in and bit his lower lip, making him growl. When she looked at him again, all fatigue left her gaze.

"Are you going to give me what I want, or am I going to have to call for Apollo?”

Ares snarled and slapped her rear. She shivered in pleasure and smiled.

"Good boy," she whispered.

Ares sat up against the headboard, giving him better leverage and easier access to her full, round rear. She slid down on him and then rocked her hips backward, grinding her pelvic bone into him. She shuddered and moaned. He slapped her butt again, forcing her hips forward. She cried out and wrapped her arms around his head, burying him between her breasts. Just where he wanted to be.

River rocked her hips back again, and he slapped her forward once more, and then her rhythm grew faster and more frantic. Ares felt the coil inside him as he drew closer to the edge again. He grabbed her hips and helped her as she rocked him inside her. Her breathing quickened, and just as he thought she was going to climax, she cried out.

"Bite me, Ares. I need you to bite me. Mark me. Make me yours."

His wolf howled in triumph, and all thoughts of Titan and Apollo getting to her first fled. In that moment, she wanted him. Him. Not them. Him.

"Tell me," he said thickly from behind his fangs. "Tell me you choose me."

She rocked back onto him again, and his climax rolled up his thighs.

She leaned into his neck, and her fangs grazed his skin. "I choose you, Ares. I choose you."

Before he could move, her fangs pierced his skin, and she cried out as she tightened around him.

Ares roared and bit her throat. His climax rushed through him in a crashing wave so intense he stopped breathing. Her blood exploded in his mouth, and his wolf howled.

His climax thickened and engorged as his knot filled her.

She cried his name as she climaxed again. Ares held her through her aftershocks until she fell onto him, limp and slick with sweat.

Her rushing heartbeat pounded into his chest as she dropped her head to his shoulder and kissed him.

He wrapped his arms around her and ran his fingertips up and down her spine. Bliss cocooned him, and he began to purr.

River sighed, and then he heard her soft snores next to his ear.

Delicately, Ares rolled them on their sides into a more comfortable position for her and watched her beautiful face. He brushed the wet hair from her cheek. They'd done it. They'd finally done it. They'd mated. She was finally his. He never knew how happy those words could make him. She was his.

"I love you, River," he whispered.

"I love you, too, Ares," she murmured.

Ares' chest squeezed tight, and a tear leaked from the corner of his eye. Everything washed away. All the pain of his past. The loss of his parents. Even his anger toward Apollo. All of it disappeared like smoke from a chimney on a winter's day. Nothing mattered anymore. Not the crown. Not the problem with the rogues. Nothing mattered but her. His River. His Beloved. His mate.

His knot barely disengaged before River woke up and called for him again. He poised over her, but she put a hand on his chest and pushed him back. She turned on her stomach and got on all fours before him.

Ares got a full view of every last swollen inch of her, and his body was ready to go again.

He positioned himself at her entrance, and his wolf clawed at his tether to be let loose.

Ares held the beast at bay as he ran his palms over her backside to her hips and gripped her tight.

"How do you want it?"

River looked over her shoulder at him.

"I want you to take me until my limbs give out, and then, I want you to take me again. And after that, I want you to take me again. And again. Until one of us loses consciousness."

Ares didn't have to be asked twice. His mate demanded he perform, so he would give her a performance she would never, ever forget.

CHAPTER TWENTY-TWO

RIVER

When her heat subsided, River couldn't even use the word exhausted to describe how she felt. Every nerve and inch of her body ached, but she felt sated in a way she'd never known. She lay in Ares' bed, staring at his glorious form. The sheet rested just above his butt cheeks, showing off his flawless, broad back and narrow hips.

Her wolf purred drowsily in a blissful state of ecstasy.

She had no idea how many times she and Ares had made love. All she knew was that their scents lingered on every surface of his room. The bed. The table. The desk. The couch. The bathroom counter. Two of the walls. The rug in front of the fireplace. Every surface of his room bore the brunt of their lovemaking over the last… however many hours.

River watched Ares' rhythmical breathing and fought the urge to touch him, but she brushed a curl from his eyes. His eyes flew open, and he grabbed her wrist.

She stared at him, and then he rubbed a circle on her skin before kissing it.

"Hello," she said.

"Hello," he replied.

She brushed her fingers down his cheek to his full lips. Need thrummed through her as she stuck her finger in his mouth, and he sucked on it before biting it playfully. Suddenly, it didn't matter how sore she was; she wanted to feel him inside her again.

Not like before. Not a frantic need from her heat. Just him. Every glorious inch of him.

Ares chuckled and kissed her. "I thought your heat was over."

She kissed him harder. "My heat is over, but my need for you never will be."

He purred. "I like the sound of that, but it makes me wonder if I didn't give you enough over the last day and a half." He crawled over her and kissed down her neck to her spine. "Which one didn't satisfy, Little Wolf?"

He licked her skin, and her body thrummed. He blew lightly on the small of her back before kissing her side.

"Was it the first time in the shower? Or the second or possibly the third?" He planted a soft kiss on her side, making her giggle.

"No, it couldn't have been those. Maybe it was that first time in my bed. It was not the second, third, fourth, or even fifth time in my bed because you told me I was spectacular those times."

He nipped her playfully, making her jump and squeal.

She looked back at him. "Tease."

He cocked an eyebrow and then brought his hand down on her rear. The sting of his palm sent shockwaves of pleasure through her, and she gasped. He leaned in close and nibbled her earlobe.

"It could have been the time on the bathroom counter. I'm sure that one wasn't as comfortable as it could have been. I should have cushioned your beautiful, tender rear with some towels, shouldn't I?"

His hand landed on her skin again with a loud slap, and River shuddered.

"Ares," she panted.

"Yes, Beloved."

"If you don't stop fooling around and take me soon, I'm going to climax without you."

He slapped her again. "You aren't allowed to until I say you can. Understand?"

River bit her lip as every nerve stood up in anticipation.

"I asked if you understood."

She nodded, biting her lip to the point of pain.

"Good girl." His hand slid over her rear, squeezing and caressing. "Now, where was I? Oh, yes. Trying to figure out where I'd failed you."

His hand slid down her backside and between her legs, where he slid his finger back and forth agonizingly slow.

"So, was it the three times in front of the fireplace?"

River fought to keep herself from shattering apart. She grabbed onto the sheets and clutched them. "Four times," she whispered. "It was four times in front of the fire."

His fingers stopped moving, giving her a moment's reprieve. "Was it four? I can't believe I lost count."

He stroked her again, and she cried into the pillow. She wasn't sure she could hold out.

"Oh, I remember now. It was the last time against the wall. I lost my grip for a few seconds near the end, and my hips shifted. I knew that one didn't feel as big as the others. That's where I failed you. I apologize. I promise not to make that mistake again. Do you forgive me?"

River's body shook as she held back her climax.

Ares slid a finger inside of her, and she bit her cheek. Her walls clamped down around his finger, and she whined.

"I asked if you forgave me," he whispered in her ear.

"Yes," she choked out.

He nipped her shoulder. "Will you allow me to make it up to you?"

"Yes," she whispered.

He slid his finger out and slid two back inside her. "I didn't hear you."

"Yes," she cried.

He kissed her shoulder. "That's my girl."

With one swift movement, he lifted her hips and plowed into her. A rumble escaped his chest as he seated himself fully inside her.

"River… You feel so amazing. I want to live inside you forever."

She shivered as he withdrew and then pistoned into her again.

"Ares."

He slid out agonizingly slowly and swirled his hips against her backside. "River?"

"Ares, please."

"Please, what?" He slid into her again.

Her thoughts no longer made sense. She couldn't concentrate on anything more than not climaxing.

"Please," she whimpered.

Ares slapped her hard and then slammed into her again. "Come on, Little Wolf, show me how much you need me."

River shuddered as Ares withdrew from her and then rocked into her hard, no longer playing, no longer teasing. Nothing but total, unbridled lust.

The pleasure wound tight inside her as he slammed into her hard and brought his hand around her waist to rub her sensitive nub.

"Show me, River. Show me how good I can give you what you need." He slapped her butt, and River screamed as her climax ripped through her.

Her entire body tensed, and Ares grabbed her by the hair and pulled her head to the side as he bit her neck. Just as she thought her climax would end, it grew even harder, and she stopped breathing.

She had no idea how many times or how loudly she called his name. She only knew that when they'd both finished, and he collapsed on top of her, they both gasped for breath. His knot filled her in a way that if he moved, she would surely climax again.

"Tell me," he said. "Tell me that you are mine."

"You know I am."

"I need to hear you say it. I know that our time together is almost up, and soon-"

She turned her face and kissed him, stopping his words. His tongue tangled with hers, and her wolf chuffed happily.

River broke the kiss and looked over her shoulder at him. "I'm yours. Today. Tomorrow. Until I die, Ares. I am yours."

A strange look crossed his face that she couldn't place. Something akin to a mixture of joy and sadness.

He rolled onto his side with her and wrapped his body around hers. "I love you, River. Until the day I die, I'll love no other but you. Not ever."

River's chest squeezed, and as she went to tell him the same, a knock sounded on the door.

"River?"

Cherry.

"What's up?"

"Do you need something to eat?"

"We'll be down in a few minutes."

There was silence for a minute. "Does that mean you're… finished?"

"She's finished dozens of times," Ares whispered.

River slapped his arm. "Yes. It's over."

"Okay. Good. I'll uh… I'll go get some food ready."

"Something sweet," River called.

"Right."

River could practically hear Cherry roll her eyes.

"Thank you, Mom," she called, but was met with silence.

River wiggled and felt Ares' knot soften. She rolled over and smacked his chest.

"That was not funny. That's my mom. What if she heard you?"

He shrugged. "This was her idea. Besides, I'm sure you and your mom have the same libido."

River's eyebrows drew together. "What does that mean?"

He smiled and ran a finger down her arm. "It means her room is right above mine, and a few nights ago, before I left… let's just say I heard Strider's name called at least half a dozen times."

River buried her face in his chest. "Ewww… yuck! Why would you tell me that about my parents? I don't want to think of them… you know."

"Having sex? Making love? Boning? Getting it on?"

"Yes. All of those."

Ares opened his mouth, but River grabbed him between his legs and squeezed. Ares sucked in a shuddered breath and shook his head.

"Of course, Beloved. I wouldn't dare ever say something like that about your mom again. But to be clear, I am absolutely sure your mother heard every single time you came. You aren't shy about yelling my name."

River squeezed him a fraction harder. Ares shuddered, and his erection grew again. He bucked his hips and grabbed her arm.

"Little Wolf, you are playing with fire."

"Feels like I'm playing with you." She squeezed even harder, climbed on top of him, and leaned in close to his ear, making sure to rub her breasts on his hard chest. "This time, it's you who doesn't climax until I say you can. Even if I get there multiple times. Understand?"

When she looked at Ares, his eyes were black, and his fangs descended.

"Yes," he ground out.

She smiled and squeezed again, making him grow thicker. "Yes, what?"

"Yes, my Luna."

She kissed him on the nose. "Good boy."

Ares growled as she lowered herself onto him.

Breakfast would have to wait. For how long was yet to be determined.

CHAPTER TWENTY-THREE

APOLLO

Apollo jumped from the SUV before it even came to a complete stop in front of the estate. Anxiety ripped at his gut. He raced up the stairs to the front door and threw it open, not even bothering to acknowledge the guards standing in the foyer. He strode up the stairs, marched down the River's door, and stopped abruptly. His stomach churned, and he fought the urge to throw up.

Cherry called him fifteen minutes before to tell him that River's need had passed and he could return. It had taken Apollo five minutes to gather his things and ten to drive to the estate. The whole ride, he'd thought of nothing but seeing River and making sure she was all right. But now, standing outside her door, he wondered. Was Ares in there? Did she still want him? Had she bitten Ares? Given him up in favor of his more gregarious twin?

His wolf paced and grumbled.

Apollo knocked on the door. He had to know. Standing in the hallway wasn't going to get him any answers.

There was a shuffle of feet, and then the door opened.

At the sight of River, his wolf jumped and chuffed. Apollo couldn't help the smile that spread across his face at the sight of her.

She returned his smile and then stepped out and hugged him.

He took in the breath he hadn't even realized he held. He rested his cheek on her head and breathed in her scent.

Ours. Our mate.

Yes.

As Apollo held her, he realized that nothing had changed between them. Everything was just as they left it. She was still his, and he was still hers. Only now, Ares' scent lingered on her as well.

Apollo waited for the punch in the gut from the realization. The fear and anger. The snarl of his wolf. But none of them came. All that mattered was River being in his arms.

"Are you going to invite him in, or are you two just going to keep hugging in the hallway?" Ares called.

River let go of Apollo and smiled before pulling him down for a passionate kiss.

"Do that in his room, would ya?" Ares said.

River chuckled and went to take Apollo's hand. He looked down at it and held out a bag to her.

"What's this?" She opened the bag and squealed. "You found it!"

"Bennett kept it safe from Silas, who tried to steal it." He smiled as she popped fudge into her mouth and groaned.

"Oh my gosh, you were so right. This is the best fudge ever. I'm going to make you go back there to get me some every month."

"I'll go every week if you want. Every day."

She smiled. "We could ride your bike up there."

"It's a date."

She reached up on her tiptoes and rubbed her nose against his. Then she took Apollo's hand and led him into her room.

Confusion scoured Apollo's body as Ares lounged on her bed, a giant tray of fruit, cheese, sandwiches, and a second tray full of candy laid out next to him.

Apollo stared at his brother, and Ares lifted an apple. "Hungry?"

"Uh… no," Apollo replied.

Ares bit into it. "Good, more for me."

What the hell was happening?

"Come and sit," said River. "We need to talk."

Apollo fought for words but couldn't find any as he watched Ares. As strange as it was to see that Ares showed none of his arrogant, selfish posturing, it surprised Apollo even more to find that even his own wolf remained calm and unaffected. That hadn't happened in Ares' presence since before their parents died.

Apollo sat on the edge of the bed, and River climbed up next to Ares and grabbed a pack of M&Ms. She ripped them open and offered some to Apollo, but he shook his head. River popped one in her mouth and then tossed one to Ares, who caught it in his.

River slapped him. "Show off."

Apollo could take it no longer. "What's happening?"

River looked at him. "You're right. This is weird for you, but trust me, it's weird for all three of us."

Ares snorted and bit into his apple. "Tell me about it. I mean, I see you, and my head says that I should want to kill you because I know you bit River and made love to her and everything, but my wolf keeps telling me that it's fine. Everything is fine, and I don't have to worry because she's ours."

Apollo nodded. "Same."

"See." River squeezed his knee. "I told you. You are both my mates."

Everything inside him told him it was the truth. She scooted closer to him and laid her head on his shoulder. Apollo wrapped his arm around her waist, waiting for Ares to say something, to threaten him, punch him, something… but he didn't.

River offered him another M&M, and this time, he took it from her fingers and crunched it between his teeth. Her finger lingered on his lips, and his body heated from her gaze.

She still wanted him. Wanted him, the way he wanted her. She was still his. He relaxed, and she melted into him.

He looked to Ares to gauge his reaction. Surprisingly, Ares remained unaffected and finished his apple. He'd never seen his brother so calm before. So… content.

"Does this mean we're… friends?"

Ares laughed. "I wouldn't go that far, but I would say that I probably won't kick your ass anymore. At least not without a good reason."

"You kick my ass? Please. You only won when I let you."

Ares snorted. "Okay, Brother. If it makes you feel better to think that, go ahead."

A strange feeling raced through Apollo. *Brother?* Ares called him brother. Ares never called him that. Ever.

His wolf chuffed and wagged his tail.

A smile traced Apollo's lips as he reached in and plucked a handful of Skittles from the tray. As he popped them into his mouth, he shook his head and looked at River.

She wiggled her eyebrows and smiled. "Are we good?"

Apollo nodded. They were good. More than good. They were… perfect.

She was perfect. Somehow, River had done what he was sure would never have been possible. She'd begun to heal the rift between him and Ares. She had tamed their beasts.

"All right," said Ares. "Time to get down to business."

"What business?" Apollo reached for a cola.

"How do we tell the Council that they don't just have one king, they have two?"

CHAPTER TWENTY-FOUR

RIVER

The entire estate bustled with activity as everyone in the household prepared for the first get-together of all Alphas of the eastern US and Canada in more than ten years.

River pulled on her dress and looked at herself in the mirror.

"Stop fidgeting," said Cherry. "Something is wrong with this damn zipper."

It had been three weeks since River's heat. The first week, she spent her days with Apollo after he worked several hours, and she spent her nights with Ares after he finished his business. Together, they'd tried to figure out how to tell the Council. Finally, they decided to send each of them a letter explaining the decision.

The second week had been spent convincing the Council that either they agreed with the twins or they would both abdicate. After all, they'd been sharing the duties for years anyway.

Ultimately, the Council decided two kings were better than no king, especially with the rising rogue problem. And because they'd already been sharing the job.

From there, the last week had flown by so fast that she'd barely had the energy to spend more than a couple hours a day with Apollo and Ares a piece. And now, as she stood staring into the mirror at the ornate ceremonial mating dress their mother had worn when mating their father, she could hardly believe everything that had happened to her in the last two months.

"Have you gained weight?" Cherry tugged on the zipper of the dress.

"What? No."

"Well, then, are you bloated and on your period because you don't fit into this dress the way you did two weeks ago."

"No, Mom, I-" River stopped. She wasn't on her period. In fact, she hadn't had a period since the week before meeting Ares.

River counted the weeks since her last period. Her heartbeat galloped, and she licked her lips.

Cherry rounded her and looked into River's face. "River. When was your last period?"

"I… I don't remember," River stammered.

"Don't lie. When, River?"

"Six weeks ago."

Cherry gasped and pressed her hand to River's belly. "That isn't all the candy you've been eating that is causing this dress not to fit, River."

River pushed her mom's hand away. Pregnant? Was she pregnant? A myriad of emotions flooded her. Happiness. Terror. Was it Apollo's? Could it be Ares'? What would they both say? Would they want her to be pregnant? Would one of them reject the baby if it wasn't theirs?

Cherry grabbed her arms and shook her. "Breathe River. If you pass out, I'll have to tell the knuckleheads why, and I do not want to be the bearer of that news."

River swallowed hard and nodded.

Cherry grabbed River and pulled her into a hug. "I'm kidding. It's gonna be fine. You're going to be fine. Ares and Apollo will be fine. Probably a lot more protective of you than usual, but they will be fine. They love you. They're your mates. It's gonna be fine, you'll see."

"Okay." River patted Cherry on the back. "I've never heard so many uses of the word *fine* before, but I get what you mean."

Cherry pushed her to arm's length. "I just want to make sure you know-"

"Everything is going to be fine?" River snorted.

Cherry shot her a look. "I was going to say all right, but yes. Millions of women have babies every day. Besides, if they aren't happy, I'll just kill them."

River smiled, and a thought drifted into her mind, and she laughed.

Cherry's eyebrows smashed together. "What's so funny?"

River laughed harder.

"What's wrong with you? Have you finally lost it?"

River continued to laugh as Cherry watched her in confusion. As tears leaked from River's eyes, she snorted and then blew out a breath.

"You want to tell me what is so hysterical?" Cherry cocked an eyebrow.

"Yeah. You're gonna be a grandma."

Cherry's expression fell.

"Grandma Cherry."

Cherry shook her head. "Nope. No way."

"Nana Cherry."

She held up her hands. "Stop."

"Grandmother Cherry."

Cherry growled. "I brought you into this world, girl, and I will stab you right out of it."

River tried to stifle her giggles.

Cherry raised her hand as if to slap River.

River opened her mouth, and Cherry cocked her hand back. River snickered and then waited until Cherry dropped her hand.

"Granny Cherry!"

"That's it. You're dead."

River squealed and laughed as she raced to the door. She threw it open and ran smack into Ares and Apollo.

The two looked between her and Cherry quizzically.

"And what are you two up to?" Ares cocked an eyebrow.

"I'm about to kill my daughter."

Apollo tsked. "Sorry, Cherry, that will have to wait for another day. Right now, we have a crowd of hungry Alphas waiting downstairs. And you know they can't eat until after we announce River's big news."

"And," said Ares. "Hungry Alphas is never a good thing."

"Yeah," said Cherry. "About River's *big news*."

"Okay," said River. "Give me just a minute, and I'll be ready. My mom just has to finish zipping me up." Without pretense, she slammed the door on her mates and rounded on Cherry.

"Don't you dare tell them. Don't you dare. This is my business, not yours. Got it?" she mouthed.

Cherry rolled her eyes. "I wasn't going to tell them."

"Promise," River whispered.

Cherry shook her head. "You're being silly."

"Promise." River took a step toward her mother.

"Fine. I promise."

River continued to stare at Cherry until her mom broke eye contact.

"Don't do that," said Cherry. "You may be an Omega, but I am still your mother."

"Sorry," River mumbled.

"Come on. Let's get you zipped before one of those two barges in here and insist on having sex with you before you head down there. Or both of them. I wouldn't put it past both of them."

Outside the door, Ares and Apollo said, "We heard that."

"Good," Cherry yelled back. "Then maybe you two will stop mounting my daughter long enough to let her get a full night's sleep."

RIVER STOOD AT THE OPEN DOORS OF THE BALLROOM, SHE HADN'T even realized existed until a few days prior. Her stomach wound in a knot.

The entire place had been decorated in warm, neutral tones, as she asked. She'd insisted that they not be overly pretentious and had instead opted for a more elegant but soothing palette. She figured that the news would shock everyone, so anything they could do to help level heads prevail was for the best.

Large candelabras lined the sides of where the chairs had been set up. A large cream carpet covered most of the wooden floor. Dozens of tables lined the walls, full of foods, desserts, and drinks waiting to be eaten. Soft classical music played in the background.

If River had picked an atmosphere for a wedding, this would

have been it. Beautiful, elegant, but simple- minus the thirty or so Alphas and their mates staring at them as they entered the doors. She glanced around and found Bianca, Cherry, and Strider sitting together, with Zeke standing nearby.

Bianca smiled and waved.

River waved back.

"Ready, Kitten?"

"Probably not."

Ares chuckled. "You still have time to tell Apollo to shove off and choose only me."

River looked up at him, and he smiled.

Apollo snorted. "You're such an ass."

Ares shrugged.

"If I forget to tell you later, you both look totally hot in those suits."

Ares growled. "Oh, I won't let you forget to tell me later."

"You don't have to tell me," said Apollo. "You can just show me as you help me out of it."

The knot in River's stomach relaxed as she laughed.

Ares and Apollo walked arm in arm with her into the room, followed by Theo and Bennett.

Everyone rose as they entered, and her dress, which had seemed slightly constricting before, suddenly felt much too tight. She forced herself to hold her head high and keep her face impassive as her gaze flicked from Alpha to Alpha.

She could do this. If Ares and Apollo could do it, so could she. It was fine. Things were going to be fine, just like her mom said. And no one could tell that she was already pregnant.

She sucked in her gut just to be sure, and together, they walked down an aisle that split the room in two.

After what felt like an hour, they reached the front of the room, where a giant red velvet blanket covered what she assumed were two large thrones. She swallowed hard and wondered when they would bring in the third throne. Or maybe there were only two thrones. If that were the case, then Ares and Apollo would sit, and she'd stand behind them. That was the only logical solution.

The trio stopped in front of the covered thrones and turned to the crowd. Theo stepped to the left a few feet away, and Bennett took up position on the right. Zeke and Santiago nodded and headed out of the room, probably to patrol with the others.

Again, a pang of guilt struck her as to why he wouldn't be with Bianca.

The Alphas each took a seat with their mates.

River tried to keep herself breathing as her gaze came to rest on her former Alpha. He watched her with a mixture of pride and surprise. She thought about waving to him, but nodded instead.

He nodded back.

Osmodius walked to the front of the room wearing a crisp black suit and white shirt. As he strode to the front, she noticed how alike his gait was to Ares'. The way he held himself. The way he dressed. All of it spoke of his noble breeding.

He gave all three of them a tight smile and a slight bow. Ares and Apollo nodded in return.

Osmodius turned to face the group. "Alphas of eastern Canada and the United States, we thank you for being here on such short notice."

River held back a snort. The trip hadn't cost the Alphas a penny. Ares and Apollo footed the bill for all of their airfare as well as their accommodations.

"Tonight is a night for great celebration. Tonight, we usher in a new era for both Lycans and shifters. Tonight, we welcome our new king and queen to their thrones. Long have we awaited this day. Ever since the death of my dear sister and her beloved Alpha, we have waited. Sometimes patiently. Sometimes, not so much. Until five weeks ago, it happened. While on a trip to New York, Prince Ares found her. Our Omega and the next Luna Queen. Princess River Whitetail."

Osmodius held out his hand to her, and River looked at it before taking it and stepping forward.

Altogether, the crowd left their chairs to kneel before her.

River swallowed hard. That wasn't what she'd expected. Looking over the audience, she realized that even Cherry, Strider, and Bianca knelt. She didn't like it.

"Please," said River. "That's-"

"Very generous of you all." Ares stepped next to her.

Apollo joined her on the other side as the Alphas lifted their heads.

"Please retake your seats," said Apollo. "Your loyalty is more than recognized and accepted."

Okay. So apparently, she still had a lot to learn about being the Luna of all shifterdom.

One by one, the group returned to their chairs.

"Now," Osmodius continued. "As you are all aware, Prince Ares is a twin. The younger of the two. Therefore, it was soon discovered that Princess River wasn't just mated to Prince Ares, but also, it seems, to Prince Apollo."

A wave of whispers crashed through the crowd.

"It is rare," Osmodius continued. "But not unheard of. Especially with identical twins. We gave Princess River one month to get to know both Princes to decide between them. And tonight, we shall learn who will become our next king."

Osmodius bowed to River before stepping to the side and out of River's line of sight.

All eyes landed on her, and she wished more than anything for a glass of water. Or a cola. Her stomach flipped at the prospect of speaking in front of so many people. This was nothing like showing her art to people. At least those people wanted to see her art; they hadn't been summoned, and they hadn't all stared at her simultaneously. They stared at her art.

"It's okay, Beloved. We're right here."

"Always, Kitten."

Both men took her hands in theirs, and she squeezed them tightly. As she looked out over the waiting crowd, the only thing she could think about was the young growing inside her already- a mom. She was going to be a mom. Was she ready to be a mom? Not that it mattered; it was happening.

She looked to Apollo. He would be a great father-attentive, kind, and fun. She looked at Ares. He, too, would be a great father-protective, fierce, and strong.

She swallowed hard and looked out over everyone. Her gaze landed on her mom.

"I am River Whitetail of the Silver Moon pack. And both Prince Ares and Prince Apollo are indeed my mates. And yes, I was told I needed to choose between them. However-"

The ballroom door crashed open, and Zeke raced in, blood splattered over his suit.

"Rogues," Zeke yelled.

River's gut plummeted. Quicker than light, Ares swooped her

into his arms. Theo growled and rushed up behind them, barking orders at the other guards in the room.

Apollo pushed in front of River and Ares with Bennett, and suddenly a panel opened in the wall behind the thrones.

“What the hell?” Apollo muttered.

The wall swung inward, and a light flickered inside.

Everyone stopped.

A scent assaulted her nose, and River's wolf went haywire.

No. No. Not him.

A prominent blond-headed figure stepped out of the hole in the wall, and Ares backed up while Apollo and Bennett shielded her from view. Her mates growled, and their fangs lengthened along with their nails.

Bennett pulled his gun, and a shot rang out, but it wasn't from Bennett. Bennett looked at River, and then a red stain spread across his chest, and his knees dropped to the floor.

River screamed, and Ares hugged her tighter.

Apollo roared and bent over Bennett, but River couldn't see his condition.

Chaos ensued behind them. Chairs crashed, and Alphas howled and roared. River looked over Ares' shoulder to see the Alphas pushing their mates behind them. Her mom jumped in front of Bianca and Strider. Zeke reached Bianca and pulled his gun. The doors burst open, and a mob of rogues prowled in.

This wasn't happening. It couldn't be happening.

River's wolf snarled and clawed to be let out.

"Isn't this a lovely party? I think I missed my invitation."

River squeezed against Ares' chest at the sound of Titan's voice.

"You're dead." Apollo jumped to his feet and leaped at Titan, but Titan raised his gun, and dozens of rogues poured out of the passageway behind him.

Titan snorted. "Wow, little brother. You finally found your balls. Did Ares give them back?"

Apollo growled and stepped forward, and River heard the click of a gun.

Her wolf cried out, and River grabbed Apollo's sleeve. He covered her hand but didn't turn.

"Why don't you put my mate down, Ares?" said Titan.

Mate? She wasn't his mate. She'd rejected him.

"You're mistaken, Titan. River belongs to Apollo and me. The deal was sealed a month ago between us."

"Wow! You two? Share? That's… new." Titan snorted.

Behind them, the standoff between the Alphas and the rogues grew tense as everyone waited.

Apollo backed up, pushing Ares and River with him as he went. They all stopped when they bumped into the thrones.

River's heart hammered, and her nails and fangs elongated.

"Leave now," said Apollo. "And we'll spare your life only."

Titan laughed, making River's gut tighten. "I'll make you the same deal. You leave now, and I'll spare you. Wouldn't you like that, Apollo? To not live in Ares' long, arrogant shadow any longer?"

Ares growled, and River pulled on Apollo's sleeve again.

Apollo looked at her, his eyes black as midnight. He touched her cheek.

A deep, sickening feeling lodged in River's gut, and her wolf whined.

Apollo kissed her palm. "I love you, River. I am yours forever. Remember that." His gaze connected with Ares. "Run."

Apollo turned and swung at Titan. Titan dodged and slammed the butt of the gun into the back of Apollo's skull.

River screamed as Ares dashed to the edge of the platform.

A shot rang out behind them, and River twisted in Ares' arms.

"Apollo!"

But the gun wasn't aimed at Apollo. Ares grimaced, his leg buckled, and he almost dropped her. Ares roared as the smell of blood tinged the air. Blood and something metal and bitter. Ares tried to get up, but his knee buckled again. He reached down, and River slid from his arms.

"Yes, run," Titan mocked. "But leave my Omega."

The bullet wound had no doubt shattered Ares' knee. River raced to a nearby curtain, ripped a strip off it, and then ran back and tied it tightly around the wound. A sickly green color mixed with black oozed out of the bullet hole.

Silver and wolfsbane.

"No." Ares tried to push her away. "Run, River. Run and don't come back. We'll find you. I promise."

River hesitated for only a second, but it was all Titan needed. By the time she'd gotten back to her feet, he grabbed her around the waist and jerked her against him.

Again, Ares fought to stand. "Let go of her before I rip your head off."

Titan snorted and shot Ares a second time.

Ares roared in pain and grabbed his shoulder.

"Stop it!" River struggled against Titan's grip and then sank her teeth into his arm as hard as possible. His blood sprayed into her mouth, and he let out a grunt. She reached for her knives, but she'd forgotten them in her room.

Titan cocked his gun again. "Stop fighting me, or I'll shoot him in the head."

River let go of Titan's arm and spat on the floor. Ares got to his feet shakily, blood soaking through his suit.

An Alpha growled, and a rogue shot forward.

"Wait!" Titan commanded.

The rogue stopped. All eyes went to Titan.

"Now." Titan turned sideways so River could see the Alphas as well as Apollo and Ares. "I'm a reasonable Alpha, so here's what we'll do. I'll let River decide if she wants to come with me or stay with the two of you."

"Fine," said Ares. "Ask her. Ask River where she'd rather be."

Apollo lumbered over to the group, blood dripping from his head down over his shoulder as well as from his side.

Titan leaned in close to River until his breath hit the side of her neck.

River froze at the memory of him on top of her, his fangs sinking into her skin, but her wolf went into a frenzy.

"Come with me, and I'll let them live. Don't, and I'll kill them both and take you anyway."

River's wolf froze.

"Look out the window."

River shifted her gaze to the large picture window. Titan lifted one finger, and a red dot appeared through the glass. It shone right in the middle of Ares' head.

"No," she growled.

Titan held up two fingers, and another dot appeared on Apollo's shirt at his heart. Apollo looked down and then to Titan. He roared and took a step forward.

Titan pointed the gun at River's head. "I wouldn't."

"He won't," said Ares. "He wants her just as bad as we do. We can take him together."

"Come on," Titan taunted. "Don't make me be a cliché and say if I can't have her, no one can. You two should already know me well enough to know that is a very real thing."

River's mind numbed, and all she thought of was the child growing inside her and her two mates. She had to protect them. She needed to save them. She didn't know when. She didn't know how, but she had to do something. She was the High Luna. It was her duty to protect them. All of them. Her mother, Bianca, Strider, the Alphas, and their mates. Everyone.

A scream rang out, and River looked over to see Zeke shoot a rogue who'd grabbed at Bianca. Cherry sliced his throat, and the rogue dropped to the ground.

"Stop!" River commanded. "Make them stop, and I'll go with you."

"What, Lover?"

"I'll go with you," River said louder.

"No." Ares took a step forward, and Apollo rushed them. The glass shattered in the window to the side of them, and a bullet ripped through Apollo's chest, and he stumbled to the ground.

"Apollo," River screamed, lunging for him.

Titan pulled her back.

Ares roared and lunged at Titan. A second shot rang out. Ares ducked, and the bullet lodged in the wall behind him.

"Coward," Ares yelled. "Scared to fight me yourself?"

Titan scoffed. "Not even close. I simply don't want to waste the energy." He leaned in and smelled River's hair. "I have a feeling I'm going to need all I have to satisfy this one."

"Let go of her," Apollo choked. "Let go of her, or so help me. I will rip out your throat and eat your heart."

Blood and poison seeped through Apollo's shirt, and River could tell by the pale tone of his skin that he was close to blacking out.

"Apollo." River struggled against Titan, reaching for Apollo. How the hell had she forgotten her knives?

"You!" Cherry leapt forward and threw a knife. It stuck straight into Titan's bicep.

He bellowed and turned.

"No!" River elbowed him in the ribs before the gun fired.

The shot caught her mom in the upper chest. Cherry stumbled and dropped.

Strider roared and raced forward.

Titan aimed again and pulled the trigger. A bullet ripped through Strider's side, and River's scream only served to echo Bianca's.

"Stop!" River commanded. "Everyone just fucking stop!"

She grabbed the knife in Titan's arm and twisted it until he let go of her.

All hell broke loose, and the rogues crashed into the Alphas and their mates. Shots rang out all around, and the scent of blood filled the air.

She raced to Cherry and grabbed her hand. "Mom?"

Blood seeped from her mom's chest, along with the same poison that leaked from Ares and Apollo.

"Mom?" River shook Cherry.

"River, run," said her mom.

She fought to maintain control as the wolves shifted and their clothes shredded. The sounds of fighting pulled her attention.

She looked at Strider. "Get her out of here. Get them all out. Get to a doctor."

River's old Alpha raced over and laid his hand on Strider's shoulder. "We have to go before we all die."

Zeke lifted Bianca into his arms. "I know a way out."

River looked at him and nodded. "Save her. Please. Save them all."

"I promise."

Strider lifted Cherry off the floor, and her old Alpha grabbed his mate. They raced through the onslaught.

Titan grabbed River by the arm and dragged her away. "Enough. Decide."

She looked over to Apollo on the ground, eyes closed.

No. Her wolf howled.

Ares and Theo fought through the rogues on the platform, but there were too many.

Tears poured from River's eyes. She couldn't lose them. She couldn't lose Apollo and Ares. She couldn't. She wouldn't be able to live if she lost them. And what about their child? She had to save their child.

"I'll go." She turned on him and steeled her gaze. "But you have to promise me. Promise that you won't hurt them if I leave with you. You won't shoot anyone else."

Titan's expression changed as she left her Omega stare on him. For a moment, he seemed conflicted, but then he smirked.

"Ask me nicely and seal it with a kiss."

He couldn't be serious.

"Show my brothers and everyone else here that you choose me, or I'll kill everyone in this building and burn it to the ground."

Tears leaked from River's eyes as she looked over at Ares on the ground with three rogues pinning him down and a fourth slashing at him.

Neither he nor Apollo would last long without having the bullets removed and the poison counteracted.

She had to save them. She was the Queen of the Lycans. She had to do whatever it took to save her family and her people.

"Please," River begged. "Please don't hurt them, Titan."

She looked at Titan full-on. His face hadn't changed from the last time she'd seen him, except for a long pair of cuts down his left cheek.

Titan turned his shaggy blond head slightly. "Do you like them, Lover? You gave them to me, remember? Not how I would have preferred you to mark me, but I've learned a lot about you these last four years, River. And one thing I've learned is that you sure leave an impression on everyone you meet."

River couldn't speak. Was it possible? Surely, a couple of scratches didn't constitute her marking him. But she'd rejected him, hadn't she?

"Confused? I was, too, at first. But then I realized I never rejected you. So you are still my mate. I took you before my little brothers even knew you existed. You belong to me."

Was what Titan said the truth?

Something deep inside told her it was. Otherwise, why would her wolf be cowering instead of fighting? And why would remnants of the red ribbon bond still be there?

Ares roared as his chest flayed open.

River let out a whine before smashing her lips into Titan's.

River's wolf snarled and thrashed, trying to break free of the red ribbon that snaked around her ankle once more.

No. Not that one. Not him.

It's the only way to save us all.

River's wolf continued to cry out in pain, but surprisingly, a soft whine escaped Titan's chest. His grip on her loosened, and his hand splayed on her back. His tongue licked the seam of her lips, and her wolf stopped cowering.

River broke away from him, confused. He gazed at her with his soft blue eyes, like when he'd pleaded with her not to reject him years before.

"There she is," he whispered. "My Luna. *My* Omega."

River's mind wouldn't work. She couldn't think. Couldn't speak. And her wolf's silence only made her that much more confused.

Titan licked his lips, and his expression hardened.

"I think we'll get along just fine, Lover."

Bile rose in her throat, and she tried to push away from him, but he was as strong as Ares and Apollo.

"Call me Lover again, and I'll make sure that both sides of your face match."

Titan chuckled. "See, I knew we were meant for each other. It's time for us to exit, Little Mate. Time for you and me to finish what we started four years ago."

"I may go with you. But I will never be your mate."

Titan smiled. "Oh, my Luna, you already are."

Titan whistled, and the rogues howled.

River glanced around frantically, her heart thundering as sweat trickled down her neck. "You promised!"

Titan nodded. "I won't hurt them. *I* won't lay a fang or claw on anyone. I can't say as much for the rogues mistreated and banished from packs worldwide."

"You bastard." River raised her hand to strike him, but he caught it and brought her wrist to his nose, smelling it.

"Sadly, yes. I am a bastard. But now, I'm your bastard."

Terror raced through River.

Titan nodded to someone behind her, and something sharp pricked River's neck. She grabbed the spot and turned to see Vanessa, a needle in hand, stepping away.

"You bitch!" River lunged at Vanessa but lost her balance as her vision went fuzzy and her legs gave out. Titan caught her and cradled her against his chest. She blinked several times, trying to clear her vision.

"Come, my Luna," Titan whispered in her hair. "It's time to take you home."

River's head lolled to the side, and before her vision dimmed, a pack of rabid rogues ripped into Apollo and Ares.

THE ALPHAS THINK THEY NEED A MATE. WHAT THEY REALLY NEED IS A QUEEN

USA TODAY BESTSELLING AUTHOR

REBEKAH R. GANIERE

CHAPTER 1

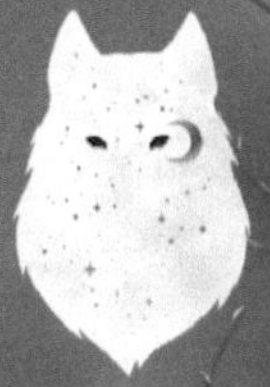

ARES

A sharp set of fangs pierced Ares's shoulder. He roared, grabbed the rogue by his jaws, and pried them apart until they snapped. Then ripped the rogue's throat out.

Another rogue took the first's place, but Ares shoved his fist through the wolf's chest and yanked his heart out.

"Ares!"

He turned as a rogue slammed a chair on Apollo's head. Ares jumped over his brother and flung the rogue across the room.

"No one kills my brother but me," he roared.

Apollo bled profusely from several places, and his skin turned ashy. Another rogue raced at Ares, but Ares caught him by the throat and ripped his head clean off. Blood sprayed over Ares and rained down on Apollo.

He scanned the room for River and caught the edge of her pink gown as Titan disappeared with her into the hallway.

All around, Alphas and Betas battled rogues. Mates hurried from the room, but several had already been taken down.

There were too many rogues. They were outnumbered at least five to one.

Ares's gut clenched. He had no idea Titan had collected so many.

Apollo dragged himself next to Ares. "What the hell are you doing? Where is she?"

Ares pointed.

"What the fuck are you waiting for?"

Ares looked at his glassy-eyed brother, who could not even sit up.

Less poison coursed through Ares' veins, slowing and weakening him. It wouldn't be long before he himself lost consciousness. He couldn't imagine how Apollo wasn't already blacked out and convulsing.

Ares' vision clouded as he inspected Apollo. No. He was not going to lose them both. Apollo may be an asshole. But he was Ares' asshole.

Suddenly, shots rang out as Theo took down three more rogues. More men rushed into the room. Bloodied and ripped apart, both his and Apollo's men tore into the room like a tidal wave. They cut their way to the front of the room, taking out rogues as they went. Theo and Santiago grabbed Ares.

"We need to get you out of here."

Ares shook his head. "We need to save as many Alphas and mates as we can. And to keep as many rogues alive as possible."

Santiago scanned the melee. "Where's your Princess?"

"Titan."

A rogue rushed them, but Santiago pulled the trigger, and the wolf dropped.

Lachlan limped forward. "You're hurt."

"Not for long." Ares leaned on Theo and took a deep breath before digging a talon into a bullet wound and yanking the metal free. He did the same with the second bullet in his knee. Damn. That one was going to take time to heal.

With the bullets free, his wolf roared and clawed to be let out. Ares wasn't sure taking out the bullets would be enough, but he had to try. He'd heal faster in Lycan form.

"Silas, Thomas, pull Apollo out now! Santiago, Theo, and the rest of you save the Alphas," Ares called. "Don't kill all the traitors. I want answers. I am going after my mate."

"I should go with you," said Santiago.

"No." Ares stripped off his shirt. "I need you to take charge here. This is something I need to do myself."

"But what if-"

"You have Apollo. So make sure he lives."

Santiago wanted to say more, but Ares growled. He didn't have time for this.

"Go! I order you." A ripple pulsed through Ares, and his Alpha command could not be ignored.

Santiago burst from his suit, fur sprouting all over his body as he leapt onto the floor.

Ares shifted and raced for the door.

"Find her!" Apollo's words echoed down the hallway as he headed for the front entrance.

He had a single goal. Find River and rip Titan apart in the process.

Dear Reader,

Thank you for taking the time to read *Alpha Claimed.* I never thought I would write a reverse harem, but when this idea came into my head, I just could not let it go.

I hope you love Ares and Apollo as much as River will.

If you enjoyed the book, please take a moment to leave a review on your favorite retailer. Your reviews make all the difference to an author and the success of books.

Feel free to take a moment and email me and let me know what you liked about the book or who your favorite character was and why. I love hearing from readers. It makes writing so much more fun when I hear from my readers.

VampWereZombie@Gmail.com

To find out more about me and my Upcoming Releases, Please Join my Street Team for Swag and Freebies.

I also love connecting with readers! Stalk me everywhere!

I look forward to hearing from you!

Rebekah R. Ganiere - BOOKS WITH A BITE

USA Today Bestselling Author

Rebekah R. Ganiere

Fairelle Series

Red the Were Hunter - Book One

Yanti's Choice - Free Fairelle Short Story

Snow the Vampire Slayer - Book Two

Jamen's Yuletide Bride - Book Three

Zelle and the Tower - Book Four

Cinder the Fae - Book Five

Belle and the Beast - Book Six

Gerall's Festivus Bride - Book Seven

Jak the Giant Healer - Book Eight

Olivia and the Giant - Book Nine (Coming Soon)

Eric's Wayward Bride - Book Ten (Coming Soon)

Wolf River

PROMISED at the Moon

CURSED by the Moon

RECLAIMED from the Moon

TAMED under the Moon

UNLEASHED with the Moon

FATED despite the Moon

FOUND because of the Moon (Coming Soon)

<u>The Society Series</u>

Reign of the Vampires

Rise of the Fae

Vengeance of the Demons

<u>The Otherworlder Series</u>

Kidnapped at Christmas

Vigilante at Valentine

Massacre at Mardi Gras

Hoodwinked at Halloween

Nightmare at New Year (Coming Soon)

<u>Immortal Monsters</u>

Dracula's Bride

Frankenstein's Bride (Coming Soon)

<u>Lycan King Wars</u>

Alpha Marked

Alpha Claimed

Alpha Queen

<u>Speed Dating with the Denizens of the Underworld</u>

Thor

Loki

Fenrir

Tyr

Happy Holiday Romances

Rekindling Christmas

Christmas Lodge

Dead Awakenings

Kissed by the Reaper

NEWSLETTER

To claim your Two FREE Books and find out more about Rebekah R. Ganiere and her other Upcoming Releases
You can Go Here:
www.RebekahGaniere.com/Newsletter

www.ingramcontent.com/pod-product-compliance
Lightning Source LLC
LaVergne TN
LVHW091111080826
845145LV00008B/1875